Havoc Begins

Havoc Begins

A Havoc in Wyoming Story

Millie Copper

This is a work of fiction. All characters, places, and incidents are products of the author's imagination or are used fictitiously. Any resemblance to actual people, places, or events is entirely coincidental.

Technical information in the book is included to convey realism. The author shall assume no liability or responsibility to any person or entity with respond to any loss or damage caused, or allegedly caused, directly or indirectly by information contained in this book of fiction. Any reference to registered or trademarked brands is used simply to convey familiarity. This manuscript is in no way sponsored or endorsed by any brand mentioned.

Written by Millie Copper

Edited by Ameryn Tucker

Proofread by Light Hand Proofreading

Also by Millie Copper

Now Available

Havoc in Wyoming: Part 1, Caldwell's Homestead

Havoc in Wyoming: Part 2, Katie's Journey

Havoc in Wyoming: Part 3, Mollie's Quest

Havoc in Wyoming: Part 4, Shields and Ramparts

Stock the Real Food Pantry: A Handbook for Making the Most of Your Pantry

Design a Dish: Save Your Food Dollars

Real Food Hits the Road: Budget Friendly Tips, Ideas, and Recipes for Enjoying Real Food Away from Home

Coming Soon

Havoc in Wyoming: Part 5, Fowler's Snare

Join my reader's club! Receive a complimentary copy of *Wyoming Refuge: A Havoc in Wyoming Prequel*. As part of my reader's club, you'll be the first to know about new releases and specials. I also share info on books I'm reading, preparedness tips, and more. Please sign up on my website:

MillieCopper.com

This apocalyptic Christian fiction book deals with not only the physical danger of surviving in a changed world but also the mental health aspect.

This is written from Laurie's point of view. You will be inside Laurie's head as she contends with thoughts of self-harm.

Chapter 1

"Don't fight it. Just relax."

"No. No, something's not right."

"Trust me," he insists. "It's fine."

"Trust you? You mean like I did last time?" I bite my lip, trying to focus, to concentrate. I know there's a problem. "He's going to run!" I shriek.

"Jerk it. Jerk it," he yells.

I give a hard upward thrust and am rewarded with my line going completely slack. I watch as the filament glistens in the sun's final rays, fluttering softly to the water.

"He snapped the line," Aaron says.

"Tell me something I don't know," I murmur.

"Are you having fun yet, Laurie?" He laughs.

I shake my head. "Oh boy! Seriously, I am having fun, even though I can't seem to land anything. Will you set up my tackle, or whatever it's called? I want to try again." I take a deep breath, then remember Aaron's day started earlier than mine. "You're not too tired?"

"Nope. I'm good. I promised you an exciting night of fishing, and that's what you're going to get."

"Will it improve after the sun fully sets?" It's dipped behind the mountain, but there's still a glow on the lake.

"Maybe. The theory is the big catfish, and maybe even larger trout, head to the shallows after it cools. But," Aaron shrugs, "I haven't noticed a huge difference between day and night fishing in this lake."

He spends several minutes digging in the tackle box, getting what he calls "a new outfit" put together.

"Did you just want a reason to play with those slimy chicken livers in the dark?" I ask, watching him fumble with the disgusting bait in one hand, a hook in the other, and holding a pen light in his mouth. It occurs to me I could at least offer to hold the light for him. Yeah, holding the light would be much better than stringing the liver on the hook.

1

Funny how I don't mind sticking my fingers in a person's mouth, but I'm not at all interested in stringing a chicken liver on a hook. I'm not interested in taking the fish off the hook either, provided I ever manage to catch one.

Aaron's good to me. We've been fishing together many times, and he knows I'm happy just to sit and hold the pole, reading a book or visiting until a fish bites. The casting and reeling in are fun, but everything else is on him.

This night fishing, though…this is new. So far, we have nothing to show for it, other than my warm and fuzzy feelings from being out here with him.

Alone.

I steal a quick glance at him. He's cute. Not like a ruggedly handsome guy, but absolutely adorable. His glasses have slipped down his nose slightly, and I watch as he wrinkles his nose to try and move them back up. His lovely, full lips join in on the action, making almost a full-face movement.

"Aaron Ogden, you sure know how to show a girl a good time." I laugh.

"Why thank you, Miss Esplin," he says with a chuckle. He gives me an amazing smile, causing my belly to do a flip-flop. "You want me to cast out for you?"

"No, I can do it. Just, you know, watch out. I'm dangerous with this hook."

"Oh, believe me, I remember." He rubs his left ear where I managed to scratch a hook across his lobe on another trip. Thankfully, it was just a graze and not a piercing.

We fish and visit until the lake is fully dark. I manage to land a nice trout. He puts up quite the fight as I bring him in, but we get him. Eventually, Aaron says, "Whatcha think, Laurie? We've caught two cats and two trout. We'll stash them in the freezer and have a fish fry after my parents get home. My mom makes the best fried fish."

"I'm still not sure about eating catfish." I shudder. "The one time I tried it, the fish tasted like mud."

"These will be better. I think you'll like them."

"Okay, Aaron. I'll try it. You must be exhausted. What time is it?"

He flicks his wrist. "It's almost midnight." Unlike most people, who rely on their phone as a timepiece, Aaron wears a wristwatch. He's an anomaly and doesn't carry a phone, doesn't even own a cell phone. He has a landline at home and says that's all he needs. Unlike Aaron, I don't own a watch but do carry a phone, which is in his pickup truck on the charger.

"So late already? You've been up since, what, six?"

"Started work at six, up at five o'clock on the dot," he says with a wink. I can't help but laugh. What a goofball. Aaron usually works four ten-hour shifts each week, Monday through Thursday, then teaches at the martial arts studio Monday through Wednesday and every other Thursday. It's a full schedule, but he handles it well. My summer job is with the same dental office that I used to work full-time for before I left for school. They're very good to me, offering me summer work when they don't really need the extra staff. Like Aaron, I work Monday through Thursday, but only six hours a day.

"I guess we should go." I try to stifle a sigh. I hate when our time together ends. Someday…

"All right, let's reel in and take off. We've got a fun weekend planned, and we'll have plenty of time together."

I stare straight ahead across the lake at a light glittering in the distance, a porch or outbuilding light on a farm bordering this large lake. I take a breath, continuing my forward stare, not daring to make eye contact. "Aaron, have you thought any more about, you know, what we discussed?"

He keeps reeling in his line, also not looking in my direction. Is he staring at the same porch light?

"Aaron?"

"Nothing's changed, Laurie," he says quietly, continuing to bring in the line. "Your folks won't be home until next summer. I think you'd regret them not being there, and we both know they'd regret it. They were very clear before they left. We all agreed we'd wait until you finish school and they get back." He grabs the hook and attaches it to an eye.

"Finish my bachelor's degree," I clarify. "You'll go with me to dental school. Then, once I finish, we move back here and I go into practice with Dr. Anderson."

I can feel him turn his whole body in my direction. I turn my head to meet his eyes.

"We *will* be husband and wife." He grabs for my left hand where my promise ring rests. I glance at his ring finger, his coordinating band missing from its spot. It's probably on his dresser at home; he rarely

3

wears it. "We'll be married, Laurie. I'll be by your side for life. I wish we would've married last summer before your mom and dad left for India, but we didn't. Now we wait—wait for your parents to return. I gave them my word. You know that's important to me, important I stick by my word."

"I know, '*Whoever keeps his word, in him truly the love of God is perfected. By this we may know that we are in him.*'" Scripture, one among many that Aaron focuses on and truly tries to live by.

"That's right, *He who says he abides in him ought himself also to walk just as he walked,*" Aaron replies—another verse he's adopted as his own.

I close my eyes and give a slight shake of my head. Yes, I know he's right. But sometimes…sometimes I don't like it much.

"So, tomorrow, do you want to go out for breakfast before our hike?" he asks, deftly changing the subject.

I play along. "You've really planned some adventures for our three-day weekend, haven't you?"

"Yep. Every weekend while you're home will be memorable. We're going to have lots of memories to carry us through when you go back to school. And then, Laurie, your parents will return home. And we will be married."

This time, my sigh is one of contentment. "I love you, Aaron."

Chapter 2

As we get close to the truck, we hear my phone ringing.

"Who'd be calling this late?" Aaron asks, worry in his voice.

"It's my mom. It's her ringtone."

By the time I get the door open, the phone is silent. It's unusual for them to call this late but not unheard of. The time difference is twelve and a half hours, so sometimes we talk at odd hours. I'm debating whether I should call them back when the phone starts playing again. They're being insistent; I hope it's not something serious.

I suck in a breath. "Mom?"

"Hey, honey. We've just heard. It's so terrible. All of us here, we're mourning with you."

"What? I don't—I'm not sure what you mean."

"Oh, I'm sorry. Were you sleeping? You don't know?"

"Aaron and I were fishing. Mom, what happened? Wait, should I put you on speaker so Aaron can hear too?"

"There's been a terrorist attack," she blurts out.

"A terrorist attack? Where? In the US?" I ask, switching the phone to speaker. Aaron wraps his arm around me, pulling me close.

"They crashed airplanes, then detonated bombs at the airports— New York, Chicago, Los Angeles, Miami—"

"Don't forget Dallas-Fort Worth," I hear Dad say in the background.

"Right, and Dallas," Mom says. "It's so terrible, Laurie."

My mind is racing. A terrorist attack, and not just one, on US soil. I try to focus as my mom continues, "They took down the planes when they were landing. And then, after the firefighters and ambulances arrived, they started blowing up the airports. The loss of life...Oh, we're just praying for everyone. We're getting ready to have a special church service."

I shake my head and wipe at my eyes, as Aaron says, "Thank you for calling, Mrs. Esplin, Mr. Esplin. We're...we're shocked. I don't...we don't...know what to say."

"I understand, Aaron. It's so terrible. We're shocked also. The whole world is likely in shock. Von's motioning me it's time to go.

5

We'll call you later. I'm so thankful you both are in Wesley where it's safe. All of the airplanes are grounded for now, just like after 9/11. A few days and I'm sure they'll get to the bottom of these attacks and things will get back to normal."

"I'm sure you're right, ma'am," Aaron says.

"Sure, Mom," I add with a sniffle.

"Oh, honey, I'm sorry to have upset you," Mom softly says. "I wish I could stay on the line and talk with you more, but…"

"Go ahead, Mom. It's fine. Maybe call me in the morning?"

"I will. I'll call you tonight, uh, tomorrow morning for you. I love you. You too, Aaron."

"Love you too, Mom." I say, as I swipe to disconnect.

"I'll turn on the radio, see what else we can find out," Aaron says, putting the fishing gear in the truck bed.

When the radio comes on, the president is speaking, "…*from Atlanta to Los Angeles International Airport crashed while attempting to land at 10:42 eastern. Frontier flight 234 from Denver to Dallas/Fort Worth crashed at 10:48. At 10:52, all flights were grounded or diverted to the nearest airport. American Airlines flight 1213 from Boston was already on final approach for its scheduled 10:58 landing in Miami. It crashed before landing.*

At 11:04 eastern, multiple bombs were detonated in or very near John F. Kennedy Airport. We expect the loss of life to be considerable. Our thoughts and prayers are with everyone directly, and indirectly, affected by this unspeakable event.

As of this moment, we do not yet know who is responsible for these cowardly acts. But I will make it my personal mission to enlist all suitable personnel in finding those responsible. God bless each of you. God bless America."

The local announcer comes on and gives a few additional details to the president's address, including highlights of responses from both sides of the political aisle. I'm disgusted that politics are even a factor during a tragedy like this.

We listen for a few more minutes before Aaron says, "I should take you home. I suspect there's a message from my folks waiting for me."

"There's a message on my phone. I thought it was probably my mom and dad, but it might be from your parents. Let me check."

I look at the missed calls, and sure enough, his mom's number is in the call log. They left two days ago for a family vacation in Wisconsin.

Aaron's oldest sister moved there last year, so the entire family, except Aaron, is doing a big get together.

I don't think the family was very happy about Aaron not joining them, but the timing was bad for his work. He's the assistant manager at an auto shop, and his boss already planned to be off for this entire month. His wife has been very sick with cancer. She's finally in recovery, and they wanted to travel. So they've taken the time to go places they've always wanted to go. Right now, they're in Hawaii. I think they go to New Zealand or Australia next.

I turn the voicemail on speaker so Aaron can hear. The message from his mom is long and rambling, interspersed with sighs and sniffles. They flew to Wisconsin and wonder if their return plans will be delayed. She ends with, "We'll make the best of it and trust in God's plan."

Aaron and his family moved to Wesley a decade ago. We met the week afterward in Taekwondo class. He was eleven, very thin and bony, and short for his age with super thick glasses. And to top it off, he was very obviously uncoordinated. Walking a straight line seemed to be a challenge.

To my fifteen-year-old self, Aaron was a nerd. A super nerd, even. I'd been in Taekwondo for about a year and a half and was wearing a green belt. We had a buddy system where upper belts worked with lower belts to show them the ropes. I was his mentor. I wasn't at all happy Grandmaster Shane paired me with scrawny geeky Aaron. I would've much rather been paired with his older brother, Andrew— my age, handsome, with amazing hair and a winning smile. I'll admit, I had an instant crush on him.

After a month, Andrew dropped out, but Aaron stuck with it. His lack of coordination, so apparent in those early classes, seemed to lessen. His recall was amazing, and he learned poomsae easier than anyone else—faster than I would've thought possible.

I was no longer his mentor. He advanced so quickly, one of the black belts took him under his wing. Even so, Aaron and I remained good friends. My senior year in high school, he was a homeschooled freshman. The summer after my graduation, we both tested for our black belts.

Aaron had changed so much since those first days. He was still a bit of a nerd, but not as thin and bony; he now looked athletic. Sinewy, even. That year, we were the same height, five foot five.

While he was still a bit of a klutz in his everyday life, once he stepped on the mat, he was amazing—crisp, yet flexible. From watching him at our practice sessions, I knew he was good, but watching him at the promotion test, I was in awe. As soon as he finished, there was zero doubt he'd earned his black belt. I passed also, but not in the majestic way Aaron did.

I sneak a glance at him; his jaw is clenched, his lips are pursed, and he keeps shaking his head. He has a death-grip on the steering wheel.

"Are you worried about your family getting home?"

He hesitates before saying, "No, they'll be fine. They can rent a car if the flights are grounded for too long. Micah will be happier if they drive anyway." Aaron gives a small laugh. Nine-year-old Micah was convinced flying was a bad idea and they'd crash. It was funny at the time, but now, after five planes have crashed in a matter of minutes...I suck in a breath to keep from crying.

Aaron comes from a large family. He's the middle child of nine. All four of the younger children still live at home in Wesley. I'm staying with them this summer while I'm home from school. Aaron has his own apartment on the other side of Wesley, near our dojang—our martial arts studio.

My parents rented out our house before they left for India. Unlike Aaron and his large family, I'm an only child. Mom and Dad would've loved to have more children, but there were complications from my birth that prevented it. I'm okay with being an only child.

Living at the Ogden home hasn't been easy. It's crazy loud all the time, and I rarely have a moment's peace. I'm sharing a bedroom with twelve-year-old Rebecca. Oh, the angst of a twelve-year-old girl! I wonder if I was ever like that. I hope not.

We turn down the driveway of my temporary home. It's a beautiful, large house with an attached double-car garage, a second story, a full basement, and a front porch large enough for two chairs and a small table. The lots in this older neighborhood are good-sized, giving them about a half an acre. In the back yard is an enormous deck, a freestanding single-car garage they use as a shed, and a well-kept lawn—Aaron's dad's pride and joy.

Always the gentleman, Aaron walks me to the front door.

"Can you...can you come in?"

He smiles. "You know I won't." I nod as he asks, "You're still up for tomorrow? I'll pick you up at..." He flicks his wrist to check the time, then winces. "How about I pick you up at nine? We'll still have time for breakfast first. I'll bring a lunch, and we'll be home in time for supper. Sound good?"

"Sounds good."

We're no longer the same height. I'm still five foot five, but Aaron's five eleven. He leans down, while I pop up slightly on my toes so I can receive his usual austere peck on the lips before he turns back to the car. He doesn't turn around as he says, "Go in the house, Laurie. You know I won't drive away until you're inside and have the door locked."

"Yes, boss," I respond, stepping into the house.

Chapter 3

Today's hike was wonderful. Even with the sadness still looming over us from last night's attacks, we're having a great time. The great time comes to a screeching halt when we return to the truck and check the radio for updates on the terrorist attacks.

While we were hiking and having fun, there was a new series of attacks. This time, bridges across the United States were damaged or destroyed. Hundreds, possibly thousands, of people died.

There are messages on my phone from both of our moms about these latest bombings. We call each of them back; both are terribly upset about what's happening. Both are also very thankful we're in Wesley where it's safe. We pick up sandwiches for dinner, eating them in Aaron's truck while listening to the radio.

I'd much rather we went to either his place or my place and watched the news on TV, but being alone on the couch isn't something we do. Sometimes the chasteness of our relationship annoys me. I'm twenty-five years old, and I can't be alone with my boyfriend? My fiancé, really. Even though I don't have an official engagement ring, I consider myself engaged. Oh, I know he has his reasons for this...caution. But still, we're both adults. I think we can control ourselves.

"What are they talking about?" Aaron asks, stirring me from my reflection.

"Huh? I wasn't listening."

"Something about people leaving their homes and being stranded on freeways." He changes the radio to a different station.

"Cities affected by today's devastation are now facing a new challenge," the announcer says. *"People are fleeing their homes, which is causing severe congestion on interstates and freeways near the affected areas. Denver, with the only bridge near us that was targeted, is in gridlock, as are the surrounding areas. Exacerbating the situation is the order from the CDC to drink only purified or boiled water until the source of the E. coli and typhoid can be determined."*

I look at Aaron with wide eyes.

He shares my wide-eyed look and gives a shrug.

The radio broadcaster lowers his voice. *"Folks, I don't want to be a fear monger, but I'd say there is little doubt our country is going to be facing many new challenges over the coming days."* The radio then switches to a sad country song.

"What's he talking about with the E. coli?" I ask, pulling out my phone to search for more info.

"First I've heard of it," Aaron says.

We soon find out this is another suspected terrorist attack. Many people are hospitalized, and there have been several deaths from suspected food and water poisoning.

"Okay, so that's definitely something that could affect us," Aaron says.

"Why would it? I mean, really—Wesley? Who'd bother with…with targeting *us?*"

"Let's check the Prospector County page, see if they give any indication if we should or shouldn't be following the CDCs recommendations."

I take a few minutes to find the correct website. Once I do, I shake my head. "Everyone on city water service is told to not drink from the tap and to boil it or use bleach or iodine to purify it. Or drink bottled water. Those on private water wells don't need to follow the guidelines. Your folks are on city water?"

He nods and asks, "This is for Wesley too?"

"Yep. Prospect, Wesley, Pryor, and all the other little towns."

Solemnly, he says, "Okay, that's fine. You'll be okay tonight. My mom should have some water in the pantry."

"She does, and there's water in the fridge already. The notice says most people can shower with the tap water but shouldn't use it for drinking, cooking, or even tooth brushing. Susceptible people—they give a list—shouldn't use it for showering or rinsing dishes either. What a mess."

"Hopefully they'll figure it out quickly. I can see how people being stranded in towns with the water polluted could become a huge deal. Do you still want to go biking tomorrow?"

I think about it for a minute before telling him I do. These are terrible events, but should they prevent us from living our lives?

Chapter 4

I've only been home a few minutes when there's a knock on the door. Did Aaron forget to tell me something? Or maybe...no, there won't be any maybe with Aaron.

I look out the side window and see a neighbor girl. She lives two or three houses down the street and is friendly with Aaron's sixteen-year-old sister, Elizabeth. What's this girl's name? Do I even know it? I take a quick look at her; she's obviously been crying.

I partially open the door. "Hello?"

"Hi, I'm Heather," she says shakily. "I live over there." She points across the street and down a house or two. "I'm a friend of Elizabeth's. We met when you first moved in."

"Okay, sure. I'm Laurie."

"Yeah, I remember. Can I use your phone to try and call my parents? I think maybe my phone is broken or something."

"Sure. Sorry your phone isn't working. C'mon in. You can use mine."

She spends several minutes dialing different numbers, or maybe it's the same number over and over. Each unsuccessful attempt seems to destroy her demeanor a little more. She's soon in full tears and flops herself onto the couch. I stand there awkwardly for several minutes as she cries.

When she seems to be getting herself together, I say, "Is there some way I can help?"

"I don't know. I'm not sure what's happening. My mom and dad went to Denver for the weekend with our neighbors."

"Oh, I see. I'm sorry they're gone with everything happening."

"It's not just that. I can't reach them. I talked to them last night after the crashes. They had just got there and checked into the hotel. They asked if I wanted them to come home, but why? The planes weren't near us, so..." She looks at me, imploring me to understand.

I do. It's just like I told Aaron, it's terrible, but it's not happening to us directly. Wesley is fine. We're safe. "Of course." I nod.

"But today..." she says, giving her nose a swipe with her arm. I point to a box of tissues sitting on the side table next to her. She grabs one, then continues, "Today the bridges were...were blown up, and *that* did happen in Denver, right where my parents are, and I haven't been able to reach them. I've been trying ever since I heard about the Denver bridge—both of their cell phones and the people they're with. It used to ring but now just goes to voicemail."

"Did you try the hotel?"

"I did," she nods. "It took a few tries, but I was able to get through. The front desk answered, but they aren't in their room. I've left messages. I just called again before I came over here. This time, the desk person sent someone out to the parking area to check for their car. It isn't there. He said phone service is spotty and I shouldn't worry. But I am. I am worried. Toby and I might go to Denver tomorrow to see if we can find them."

Whoa. Not a good idea. I try to keep my face even as I say, "The roads are clogged."

She makes a face. "Going out of Denver, but we want to go *into* Denver." She says it like I'm a huge idiot.

I form my lips into something resembling a smile. "Not sure it matters much. Who's Toby? Your boyfriend?"

"No. Ick. Toby James? His parents are with my parents. They live across the street from us, two doors down from you."

I must have a blank look because she says, "He has a bad zit problem."

Oh, yes, him. I nod. "I've met him."

"Right, so we thought..."

Her voice fades off.

"Where would you look? If they aren't at the hotel, where would they be?"

"Shopping, the spa, the Rockies game—that's tonight. Then some theater thing tomorrow night. Those were the things they were going to do. But what if they..." Her lip quivers, and her eyes fill up again. "What if they were on the bridge?" she whispers.

I gasp. Oh no. Surely, they wouldn't have been on the bridge at the exact moment it exploded. I search my memory for what was said about the bridge in Denver. The explosions produced varying degrees of destruction, with some being nearly total to others with possible structural damage, not confirmed, so they're closed as a precaution.

"Speer Boulevard Bridge, the one in Denver, was listed as destroyed," she says, answering the question I didn't ask out loud.

13

"And you think—"

"It's the only thing that makes sense. They were on the bridge or near it, and now they're at the hospital or trapped or…worse. So Toby said we could go and find out."

"I don't think you should. Denver will be too much of a mess. I'm sure they have help lines set up for this. Let's find out."

"You mean like some kind of hotline listing the injured or…"

"Probably something like that. If they don't have it all, um, put together, they're working on it. I'm sure they are."

She nods, a hopeful look on her face. "Should we have Toby come over too?"

I think about it for a second before saying, "Why not?"

She calls him, and he shows up within five minutes. He does have a serious acne problem, most of his face is riddled in active lesions. Dr. Pimple Popper would have a heyday with him. In addition to his unfortunate acne situation, his hair is in need of a washing, and his thick glasses are smudged and have slipped off the bridge of his nose.

He pushes them up as he tells me hello. The smile he gives me seems to erase the other issues, and I can see an attractive young man underneath all the…other stuff. Also, with the way he looks at Heather, I can see he has a huge crush. I wonder if she notices it.

We spend a good hour on the internet and phone, going through the process—and getting nowhere. Well, no definitive answers anyway. If they can't reach their parents by Monday morning, then they can file an official missing person report.

Pretty much, they're told what the desk clerk at the hotel said—cell phone and landline services are spotty. They're probably somewhere and fine, unable to reach their hotel due to the traffic issues, so they're staying elsewhere. They're sure to call when they can.

The children leave shortly afterward. I make them promise not to go to Denver to look on their own. They agree. I hope they're as committed to keeping their word as Aaron is. I suspect they're not.

Chapter 5

The knock on the door starts off light but intensifies rapidly. I'm still tying my robe as I peer out the side window. The sun is up just enough I can make out the person banging at this way-too-early hour.

It's Heather, the girl from last night. She's bouncing up and down on the porch, grinning from ear to ear.

Before I have the door opened more than an inch, she cries, "They're fine! I got a text saying everything is fine. Toby's parents too."

"That's wonderful, Heather. Does Toby know?"

"Yes, I called him. My parents said his parents sent him the same text, but they asked me to tell him in case it didn't go through. It was like the hotel clerk said: they couldn't get back to their hotel. They stayed in a church shelter last night. They don't know when they can get home, but they're fine. They're okay. I sent them a text back but haven't heard from them yet. At least I know."

"I'm so happy for you. And Toby too."

She lets out a big sigh; her entire body seems to relax. "I think I'll go home and sleep for a while. I didn't really sleep last night. I was so...you know, worried."

"Of course, it'll be good to get some sleep. Would you like to come over for dinner tonight? Bring Toby too. I'll ask Aaron to join us, and we'll grill burgers or something. We can celebrate."

"Sounds good. What time?"

"Around six?"

"Okay, yeah. I'll tell Toby. Umm, you know, Toby and I, we aren't—like, our parents are friends, but we just know each other."

"Sure. I get it."

She smiles and says, "I'm sure he'll want to come to dinner. See you then."

I'm dressed and ready to go when Aaron shows up around 7:30 with bagels and coffee. While I can drink coffee pretty much all day, Aaron allows himself one cup only and always before 9:00 am.

"Good morning, beautiful," he says, giving me a hello kiss. "I'll be right back." When he returns, he's carrying two five-gallon jugs.

15

"What's this?" I ask.

"Water. I boiled it for you, to make sure you have enough. I thought we could fill up any empty jars around here with them, then I'll take at least one of these containers back with me so I can refill it. I'll make sure you don't run out."

My heart melts at his thoughtfulness. Things like this are why I love him. "How early did you have to get up to boil and cool this water for me?"

"Not too early. I boiled some of it last night. It was cool this morning. This jug I did this morning," he motions to one of them, "so it's still warm. We'll empty the cool one out."

"Thank you, Aaron."

"You're welcome." He leans in to give me a peck. I'm slightly surprised when his lips linger a split second longer than usual.

A flutter runs through me. It's not like Aaron's my first boyfriend and I haven't been kissed before. I have, and then some. More than "and then some," even. But it's different with Aaron.

We were friends for so many years. After high school, I started working for Dr. Anderson. At first, it was just front office stuff, but then he trained me to assist with simple dental procedures. During that time, Aaron and I were assistant instructors at the dojang two nights a week. Master Shane, now retired, was still working full-time. Along with two other black belts, we'd help cover when his rotating schedule didn't work with teaching.

Aaron and I going from students to teachers was not without slight growing pains. As an upper belt, I'd often lead the warmups and help train brand new people, but to actually be considered an instructor was slightly different. I had no problem learning to call Master Shane *sir*, *Master*, or *Grandmaster* when I wanted to be properly formal. Even now, I don't call him Bill. Aaron does, but not me.

But calling Aaron, who's four years younger than me, *sir* and *Mister Ogden* wasn't easy. And calling him *sir* when he was in charge of the class would sometimes make me laugh—of course, I'd try to hide it so the other students didn't catch me. He had similar problems with calling me *ma'am* or *Miss Esplin*.

Teaching together was fun because we both had slightly different strengths. That year, Aaron started focusing on Yongmudo also; a Korean martial art primarily focused on self-defense. Even though there's some crossover, it's a different discipline than Taekwondo. He

16

was essentially starting from scratch, even beginning at the white belt level, and earning new belt colors as he promoted. He was super busy with practice three or four nights a week, then going to regional tournaments any time there was one within driving distance.

Work, Taekwondo, and the occasional tournament was enough for me. I didn't want to add in another discipline. Plus, I had a social life, including a few boyfriends. When I was nineteen, I started dating Michael. Oh my, what a disaster that turned out to be. I dated Grant after Michael, which wasn't much better. Then Rudy, a good guy but not for me. He's now engaged to my friend Penny. There were a few others mixed in among the major boyfriends, but they weren't serious. And I wasn't Aaron's first girlfriend either. Which is the essence of our platonic commitment.

"So, Laurie, would you mind if we rode around the lake instead of going up into the Big Horns?"

"That's fine, but I thought there was that new—what'd you call it? 'Gnarly trail just ripe for shredding.'"

Aaron laughs. "I don't think I said it quite that way."

Aaron's dad is passionate about outdoor sports, including mountain biking, backpacking, and skiing. He passed his passion on to the children. His latest thing, which Aaron's brother Gabe also enjoys, is trail running. Aaron's tried it once or twice but doesn't have the same ardor yet. But the other things, he's really embraced. He says they help him improve his martial arts skills by working different muscles and requiring balance.

I have to admit, while I enjoy the outdoorsy stuff, I only do it because Aaron loves it. During the school year, other than twice weekly Taekwondo practice, I'm a couch potato. And I kind of like it.

"We can skip the ride if you think we should," I say. "Oh, that reminds me. I can't believe I forgot to tell you about Elizabeth's friend Heather."

He gives me a blank look.

"You know, the girl living down the street?"

He shakes his head.

I stifle a sigh and say, "Shoulder-length brown hair, cheerleader type."

"The one Toby James has a crush on?"

17

I knew it! "Yep, that's the one. She and Toby were both here last night. Their parents went to Denver together, and they couldn't reach them. Heather was sure they were killed in the bridge collapse."

His face instantly turns to worry.

"They weren't," I quickly add. "She came over this morning and said she got a text from them. They're fine." I meet his eyes and nod, watching as his face relaxes.

"That's good. While my parents don't really socialize with the Morgans and the Jameses, they're friendly."

"It's probably going to be a few days before their parents can get home, you know, with the traffic and other troubles, so I invited them over for dinner tonight. I thought we could grill."

"Sure, that's a good idea. Let's check my parents' freezer for something we can thaw for tonight."

Chapter 6

"Whew. I'm glad we didn't go to your gnarly new trail," I say, after gulping down half of a second water bottle.

"This was a good ride. The washboard and the rock garden always make for a fun time," Aaron says, before squirting water over his head. When he shakes his head like a dog, we both get wet.

"Hey!"

"Oops." He grins. "Thought you might need a cool down."

"Oh yeah?" I ask, making my water bottle squirt him like a hose. He grabs me with one arm and dumps the rest of his bottle over my head. I squeal and then move far enough away to give him another hose-like squirt. "You're going to get it, mister!"

After several more minutes of figuring out how to soak each other with water, we're both laughing and tired again—and also realize we need to stop what we're doing before we cross a line we've agreed not to cross.

"We'd better get going," I say. "Heather and Toby will be over at 6:00."

"Okay. I'll drop you off and then go to my house and get cleaned up. It's a little after 4:00. With drive time, I should be back to your place by 5:45."

We secure the bikes and start the truck. I reach for the radio. "Let's see if there are any updates on the attacks, or the water and food issues."

"…in addition to financial institutions going down, social media giants Facebook and Twitter, along with YouTube, Google, and Yahoo, are unavailable, due to what is believed to be a distributed denial-of-service taking these out.

"With so many people turning to social media and online searches to stay up to date on the latest news, this is causing extra panic. The affected sites hope to resolve these outages as soon as possible. 911 operators are being inundated with calls reporting downed statuses of websites. Please do not call 911 to report any websites being down. Please reserve 911 for true emergencies only."

"People are calling 911 because they can't get on Facebook?"

"Wait a minute," Aaron says, motioning me to stay quiet.

"Again, we're receiving reports of dozens of financial institutions offline by what is believed to be the result of a malware cyberattack. The affected banks are unable to offer any online services, which has shut down credit and debit cards, online banking, and ATM machines. While it is a Saturday and most bank branches are closed, people are prevented from withdrawing money directly from branches since the computers cannot be accessed for these records. We've been assured these attacks are being addressed and services should soon return to normal. We'll provide updates to this developing story as more information becomes available."

"Well, bummer. No internet and no shopping."

"I think it might be more than that, Laurie. Everything is computerized. If there's a cyberattack, it could affect more than the internet and credit cards."

"Like what?"

He chews on his lip for a moment. "I'm not sure, maybe nothing more."

"What aren't you telling me, Aaron?"

"You know, I'm probably just paranoid. It's just, when they say cyberattack and malware, I start to wonder. I'm sure it's nothing."

One of the things I love about Aaron, and also hate about him, is the way his brain works. Sometimes people don't expect much of him. After all, he's a simple mechanic. He didn't go to college and doesn't even have a high school diploma.

He was homeschooled from kindergarten through high school. When he turned sixteen, he started working at the auto shop. He loved it and was soon working full-time while continuing his studies in his off hours, at his mom's insistence. Eventually, his mom unofficially graduated him and he took his GED. He was the first of his homeschooled siblings to not go on to college. The four older ones have a similar higher education path as I do. We started our college careers at the local community college, then went on to universities. Unlike me, Aaron's siblings have already completed their schooling and have excellent careers.

Secretly, I think Aaron's mom was disappointed he didn't go the college route, but he loves being a mechanic. And the fact he's a mechanic has no reflection on his intellect. He's nothing short of brilliant. He has almost total recall and a unique, analytical way of

20

looking at things. I also know he'll tell me when he's ready, if he determines there's anything to tell.

As expected, Aaron shows up at 5:45. I'm putting the finishing touches on a spaghetti salad; a yummy concoction I had at a restaurant in a nearby town and have recreated at home. Spaghetti with an Italian dressing, bell pepper, cucumber, red onion, chunks of cheddar cheese, and halved cherry tomatoes.

A few minutes after 6:00, I open the door for Heather and Toby. "Hey, you two. You both look considerably better than last night."

"I slept most of the day," Heather says.

"Me too," Toby agrees.

"Do your lights work?" Heather asks.

"What? Why wouldn't they?" I flip on the switch in the kitchen. Nothing. I flip it up and down a few more times.

"See? Our power is out too. You didn't know?"

"When did it go out?" I search my mind, trying to remember if the refrigerator light worked when I pulled the produce out. I open the fridge door to check—no light. The Ogdens have a simple battery-operated wall clock in the dining room and a few others scattered about the house. Part of their homeschooling requirements is being able to tell time on a real clock. As far as I know, the only electrical-dependent digital clock is the alarm clock in my room.

Heather shrugs. "I was blow drying my hair, maybe half an hour ago? Weird you didn't know."

"Yeah, I guess it is."

"Phones aren't working right either," Toby says. "They said on the radio that some carriers are down completely and others are working part of the time. Is your phone working, Heather?"

She nods. "I was texting my parents right before I came over. They said the power is out in Denver too."

"I sent a text to my mom but haven't heard back," Toby says. "Not sure if it went through. And I tried to call, but it didn't work."

Aaron slides open the patio door. "Hey, Toby. Nice to see you. Heather, you're a lot older than I remember."

She blushes. "I'm the same age as Elizabeth."

"She's older than I think she should be too," Aaron says with a laugh. Heather's blush intensifies. Toby may have a crush on Heather, but I suspect Heather has a crush on Aaron. Understandable. He's her

21

friend's older brother. I stifle a giggle, thinking how I'm going to have to tease Aaron about this later.

"The power is out," I say, "and they say the phones aren't working right."

He's instantly solemn as he sighs and says, "I was afraid of that."

I give him a questioning look. He shakes his head and mouths, "*Later.*"

I walk to the table and pick up my cell phone. "I think I'll try to call my mom." I try several times but the call won't connect. I send her a text asking if she can call me. It's still early in India, so it might be a while before she's up and around.

We're on the back deck finishing up dinner when we hear someone rattling the gate to the backyard. "Yo, yo. Y'all back there?"

"Who's that?" Heather whispers.

"Probably just one of the neighbors," I say, not recognizing the voice, but who else could it be?

I stand to walk to the gate, when Aaron wipes his mouth and says, "I'll check."

He walks around the corner of the house. "Hey, dude," the voice from the gate says. "Thought we'd let you know about the party tonight. With the lights out, we thought it'd be a good time for a bonfire. It'll be right at the end of the cul-de-sac."

"Okay, sure. I'm Aaron Ogden. I don't think we've met."

"Yeah, dude. I've met your old man. Name's Jeremy, and this is Chuck."

"Dude," a second, very deep voice says.

"Thanks for the invite," Aaron says. "I appreciate it."

"You're welcome, man. Be sure to bring your girl. A pretty girl always livens up a party."

"Right," Aaron says.

"Later, friend," the deeper voice says.

Aaron comes back to the table, sitting down without a word.

"So there's a party tonight?" Heather asks, more excited than I think she should be.

"Sounds like it." Aaron nods.

"You two are going to go, right?" Toby asks.

I have to admit, after these few days a party does sound good, but distasteful at the same time.

22

Aaron gives me a long look and a slight shake of his head. "I'm not sure. Those guys...I don't think a bonfire sounds very smart. Not while the power is out anyway."

"What's the power being out have to do with a bonfire?" Heather asks sweetly, batting her eyelashes to add to the effect.

"Maybe nothing," Aaron says. "But I seem to remember reading something about a power outage and a fire starting and there being a problem with water for the firefighters. Which makes me think, maybe we should store some water."

"Store some water?" I ask dumbly.

"Yeah. I don't think Wesley has a gravity-fed system. Well, it is to a point. The water is pumped from the reservoir outside of town and into one of the water towers. The water from the tower uses gravity, but a pump puts the water into the tower.

"No electricity, no pump. Of course, I'm sure they have a generator they're using, so everything is fine now, but...I just think it'd be smart. You two also," he directs his instructions to Toby and Heather. "Fill up containers and the bathtub. We already talked about boiling your water."

"Right. I'll do that when I get home," Heather says, with those eyelashes fluttering again. "It grosses me out to think our water might be dirty. The water in the containers, use it for drinking?"

"Drinking, cleaning, bathing. The water in the tub can be used for flushing the toilet," Aaron says.

"I'll help you get your water, Heather," Toby says. "We can do that and then I'll take you to the party if you want."

Aaron shakes his head but doesn't disagree with Toby and his suggestion of the party. While Aaron's his own person and makes his own decisions, he never browbeats others into believing or thinking the same as he does. He doesn't do it to me either, one of the many things I appreciate about him. I know he isn't always in favor of some of the choices I make, both in the present and in the past, but he also never rebukes or passes judgment. Besides, it's not like Aaron doesn't have his own past.

"Oh, well, I probably don't need any help, Toby," Heather says. "Thanks anyway. I guess I'll get going. Oh, unless you'd like some help cleaning up, Laurie?"

I wave her away.

"I'll walk you home anyway," Toby says.

23

After we fill up the bathtub and several containers, Aaron helps me with the dishes.

"So, you knew the electricity was going to go out?" I ask.

"I didn't know. But I thought it might. Remember that thing a few years ago in Ukraine when they had a cyberattack?"

I have no idea what he's talking about. "No."

"Yeah, well, it wasn't too big of a deal, and they got it under control pretty quickly, but the electricity went out for a few hours, so…" He shrugs. "Do you…uh, I'm worried about the bonfire. I want you to promise me, if anything seems dangerous, you'll call me immediately."

"Dangerous? It's a block party. Why would it be dangerous? Oh, you mean in case the fire gets away from them?"

"Not just that. I haven't seen those guys here before, but I heard from my dad about some guys renting the house at the end of the block. You know, the Johnston house?"

"Sure, I know about it being rented out, and I also heard about the people renting it. I've seen them too. They're just wannabes."

"Wannabes?"

"Yeah, they want to be gangsters, but they're not, so they just pretend. Besides, we don't have any real gangs in Wesley."

"I'm not so sure about that. Master Shane says there's been lots more burglaries and things lately. He said the sheriff department is getting close to figuring out who's behind it, and it seems like it might be fairly organized. Plus, we've had a drug problem for years, you know that."

Master Shane, retired sheriff deputy, is still very much in tune with what's happening in the county. I have no doubt he knows what he's talking about. And I definitely know about the drug problems Prospector County has.

"So, uh, just call me if you need me, okay? Don't worry about the time or anything."

"The phones aren't working right, remember?"

He looks very concerned for a moment, before saying, "Right. I forgot. Probably everything will be fine. Just in case, let's grab a couple of things from the gun safe."

I roll my eyes. "Not necessary."

"You're probably right, but I'd feel better knowing you had a weapon in easy reach."

24

"I *am* a weapon, remember?" I give him an exaggerated wink and a pretend karate chop to his neck.

"Oh, yeah. No doubt about that. C'mon, Laurie."

"Yes, fine." It's not that I have a problem with the idea of having a gun. My guess is most Wyoming kids learn to handle a firearm at an early age. I'm not any different. My dad taught me, and I've shot several types of rifles, handguns, and even shotguns. Shooting at targets is fun. I've never been hunting, though, or seriously considered using a gun for self-defense.

Aaron retrieves a shotgun and handgun from the gun safe; I've shot both before. "How about putting the handgun on your nightstand? Maybe the shotgun in the hall closet?"

"Why not? I kind of think you're being a little—"

"Paranoid? Ridiculous?"

Yeah, those were a couple of the words I was thinking. But now…I soften my tone. "Cautious. You're being cautious, and I know it's because you care for me."

"Not just care for you, silly. I love you."

After making sure I have ammunition and the guns are within easy reach, he gives me my goodbye peck.

Chapter 7

I'm almost asleep when the revelry starts, the beat of the music practically vibrating the windows. At first, I snuggle down under the covers and try to ignore it. As the party intensifies, I realize ignoring it isn't going to work. I try to read, which is impossible with everything going on. Finally, since I can't sleep, I decide I might as well check it out.

I dress in jeans and a T-shirt, then slip on a pair of flip-flops, pulling my long hair into a high ponytail. My hair's naturally a chestnut brown color, but I dye it lighter and add highlights. I like the depth and extra shine the fake color gives. During the summer, the highlights get even brighter from the sun. Hopefully Aaron's wrong about the water problem. Not being able to wash my hair would be an issue—a serious issue.

The bonfire lights up the end of the cul-de-sac. There's a whole lot more people than just those who live on our little street. I stay on the sidewalk, straining by the light of the fire to recognize anyone. After a minute or so, I see Heather talking to a girl around Aaron's age, who I also recognize.

Heather sees me and gives a small wave. She's glancing around, maybe looking to see if Aaron's with me?

Walking toward her, I return her wave. Toby is in a group standing near Heather, his eyes on her. When she waved at me, he made a point of searching out the recipient of her gesture. I give him a nod and smile.

"Hey, Laurie," Heather says. "Thought you weren't coming?"

I shrug. "Kind of hard to sleep with all the noise, so I figured, why not?"

"Where's Aaron? He didn't come with you?"

"Aaron went back to his place, not long after you left."

"Oh? He doesn't sleep over?"

I respond with a smile and turn to the other girl. "You look familiar, but I can't remember your name."

"I'm Meadow. Meadow Reid. We were in high school together. Well, not really together. You were a senior when I was a freshman,

26

but we had band together. I played the clarinet. Do you still play the flute?"

"Of course, I thought you looked familiar. No, I haven't picked it up in years, not since high school."

"Yeah. Same. I actually quit band my junior year. There were too many other classes I needed to take."

We start talking about the different people we know. Surprisingly, Heather also knows a lot of the same people, having an older brother a year younger than Meadow. He lives and works in St. George, Utah. Heather says his girlfriend is expecting a baby any day.

"So you're going to be an aunt. That's exciting," I say.

"It is. It's a little girl. I'm not sure how much we'll see her, though. Mom hopes he'll move back up here, but it's not very likely. He has a pretty good job, and his girlfriend's family is all there, so..." She shrugs.

We talk about the cyberattacks and how freaky it is the phones and lights don't work. Heather also tells Meadow about her parents being in Denver, but she totally downplays those first few hours of fear. I can't say I blame her.

"Well, hey there, you beautiful ladies," a deep baritone voice says.

"Hey, yourself," Meadow says with a huge winning smile. "Chuck, do you remember Laurie Esplin? She was a senior when we were freshmen."

I look over Chuck. He's one of the guys renting the Johnston house and, judging from his voice, one of the ones at my gate earlier, but I don't know him from high school. In fact, I'd have pegged him as older than me.

He has a very high hairline and prominent forehead. Instead of hiding this feature, he plays it up with a pomp cut, shaved on the sides and long on top. He's wearing so much mousse, or whatever it is, to hold his hair in place, I suspect even our strong Wyoming winds wouldn't dare affect it. His hair is so perfect. He probably spends more time in front of the mirror than I do!

Clad in a white T-shirt with the left sleeve rolled up to hold a pack of cigarettes, Levi's, and black combat-style boots, he reminds me slightly of John Travolta in Grease. Overall, it's a rather impressive look. I guess this is what the fashion-conscious wannabe gangsters in Wesley wear to a bonfire.

"Well, hey there, Laurie Esplin. Where have you been all my life?"

Seriously? Is this a pickup line? I mumble something while Meadow and Heather both laugh.

"You're the one who invited us to the party," Heather says. "At least, I'm pretty sure it was you. We were having dinner in the backyard. I think I heard your voice at the gate."

"That so?" he asks. "Jeremy and I did go out and personally deliver invitations. But I'd remember talking to women as beautiful as you two."

"Oh, we didn't talk to you. Her boyfriend," Heather jerks her thumb toward me, "you talked to him. But he's not here. Just us." She gives him a big smile.

"Well, then. How about we get you three a drink. Meadow, I'm surprised you don't have one already."

"Beer, Chuck? Yuck." she answers.

"Oh, we have other things. Just not out for the general public. The good stuff is hidden for special people."

"Uh, I think we'd better get going, Heather. Don't you?" I ask, touching her arm.

She looks at me like I have three heads. "You can go. I'm staying."

"No reason for either of you to go," Chuck says. "We have plenty of booze to go around. Besides, haven't you heard? It's the end of the world as we know it, and we should be feeling fine."

Chapter 8

When I wake up Sunday morning, my head is pounding and fuzzy. I turn the light on in the bathroom. Nothing. I flip it up and down several times before I remember the power is out. I squeeze my eyes tight. Coffee. I'm really going to need some coffee.

At least the water is still running, but even after a good minute, it never gets warm. I turn it off and lean against the wall, massaging my temples. I guess that makes sense, the hot water needs electricity to work. I feel like a dork for not thinking of this sooner.

Hot water or not, I need a shower. I stink like bonfire and booze. I only had two rum and cokes, but whoever was making them wasn't measuring—they were way stronger than I'm used to. The hammering in my head confirms I should've stopped with one.

It's 8:30 now. Aaron will be here at 10:00 to pick me up for church. During the school year, I don't attend church. I know I should, and my parents definitely think I should, but I'm so busy, finding a new church is low on my list of priorities. My family and Aaron's family used to attend the same church. About five years ago, my parents and I started going to a different church, which is now sponsoring their India mission.

Mom and Dad's mission focus is on ministering to widows. In India, widows are often cast out and end up homeless, considered pariahs. My parents are working with an established church, which owns several homes specifically for these banished women. Mom says it's rewarding and heartbreaking at the same time.

Aaron's parents left the church a few years back. They were essentially forced out under extremely sad circumstances. The church the Ogdens attend now is a small group that meets in a classroom at a private school. The new church, and specifically Pastor Robert, have been good for Aaron, allowing him to overcome a lot of heartache.

I need to figure out how to clean up and get coffee—lots of coffee—before Aaron shows up. I also need to put my phone on my car charger. The battery is seriously low.

The gas still works, so I use the stovetop to heat water for washing. It's not a shower by any means, but I feel better. The three Tylenol I downed make a substantial difference, and my need for coffee is helped by a jar of instant lurking in the back of the kitchen cupboard. The flavor is pretty bad, but the caffeine jolt helps.

When Aaron arrives at five of ten, I'm looking pretty good, if I do say so myself. I guess Aaron thinks differently.

After kissing me hello, he says, "So you went to the bonfire?"

"How'd you know?"

He gives me a half smile. "You aren't quite your chipper self."

"Chipper? Have you been taking vocabulary lessons from your dad?" I ask with a slight laugh.

"Guess so." He smiles his sideways smile.

I tell him about the party and seeing people from school. Since he was homeschooled, he didn't run in the same circles as most public school kids and isn't sure he knows them, but he listens and nods appropriately.

After a few minutes, he says, "The phones still aren't working this morning. I heard on the radio both the phones and power outages are even more widespread than yesterday. Might be a while before either are fixed for us."

"Really? How can that be?"

"It's pretty bad, with the malware and everything."

"I'm sure, in today's world of technology, they'll be able to figure something out."

"Maybe. But I think the world of technology is part of the issue." He flicks his wrist to look at his watch. "We'd better get going."

Our church service elaborates on everything happening in the past few days and ties it together with scripture. Personally, I think it might be a bit of a stretch in some cases. I freak out slightly when, near the end, as Pastor Robert is wrapping things up, he says, "It wouldn't be a bad idea to stop at the grocery store, buy a few things to hold you over."

Afterward, I ask Aaron if he thinks that's necessary. He shrugs, but the lady behind us says, "Probably a good idea. You've heard the phrase 'there are only nine meals between mankind and anarchy?'"

I look at Aaron; he shakes his head.

"I don't think so," I say.

She nods. "The theory is grocery stores only stock enough food for three days. They receive deliveries several times a week, so they don't need more than that. But what happens if a delivery can't be made?"

I start to answer as she plows on, "They run out of food. No food, and people go a little nuts. Law and order break down and you have anarchy. See?"

"Okay," I say.

"That makes sense, Mrs. Holland," Aaron replies. "Thank you for telling us."

"Mm-hmm," she says. "You, Aaron Ogden, are already skinny as a rail. You can't really afford to be missing any meals. Now you take care."

I stifle a laugh at the look on Aaron's face. He's very trim, but I don't think of him as skinny, and he definitely doesn't think of himself as skinny. He's fit and muscular, without carrying extra fat. With as athletic as he is, it wouldn't be able to stay on. But she does make a good point, Aaron has a voracious appetite. Again, because of his athleticism, he needs the fuel for his body.

I also choose to ignore how Mrs. Holland doesn't comment on me needing to be sure I don't skip any meals. Humph.

We visit with a few more people on our way out. We're all upset over the attacks of the last few days, but other than Mrs. Holland, no one else seems to think extra shopping is needed.

We're going on a short hike this afternoon, the last day of our special three-day weekend. Sure, we have another weekend in just a few days, but Aaron's parents will be home and we won't have the time to ourselves—at least, we hope they'll be home. When Aaron talked to them yesterday, they hadn't decided if they'd drive home or wait for the airplanes to be ungrounded. Of course, he talked to them early in the morning, before the cyberattacks. I wonder what they're thinking now?

"Laurie," Aaron says, "there might be something to the food and anarchy thing."

"How do you figure?"

"A lot has happened in the last few days. Airplanes are grounded. Bridges were blown up. Interstates are clogged. And now, the power and phones are out. How do you think trucks can bring groceries?"

I start to answer, then hesitate. He might have a point. "How does the power outage affect groceries?"

"Some gas stations aren't working. No power means no gas. I checked before going to your house this morning. All three in Wesley are still working, but they're limiting people to a ten-gallon purchase,

31

cash only. Let's drive by the stations and the grocery stores, see what they look like now."

I shake my head. "I guess, if you think we must."

"Humor me, Laurie," he says with his lopsided smile.

There are crowds of people at both grocery stores, and the gas stations have increased their prices and lowered the amount they're giving people. It's now fifty dollars for five gallons. "What about the other gas station?" I ask.

"What station?"

"The one on the other side of the college."

"Oh, yeah. I forgot about that one. I didn't go by there this morning, so I don't know if it's open. But I think we should get our five gallons for my truck, then go get your car."

"Fifteen gallons," I say. "I have some cash, and my car is almost empty."

"They're only allowing five gallons."

I try not to sigh or roll my eyes. "We can go to each station and get the amount each of them allows. Don't you need more than five gallons?"

"I filled up yesterday morning before we went riding. Five is probably fine," he says as he pulls into a station.

"Well, I need more than five," I mutter.

It takes twenty minutes before we get our fuel. We go from there to my house and get my car. "I'm going to check out the station by the college. Maybe other people forgot about it too."

I'm super excited when we pull up and see there isn't a line. Then I see the NO GAS sign. Bummer. Much to Aaron's dismay, I go to get my five-gallon limit at the other stations.

"Should we buy some groceries?" I ask. "Your parents' freezer is still pretty full from last year's hunting season and all those deals your mom finds, so we have food."

"Their freezer..." His voice fades away, then he says, "The freezer needs electricity."

"Oh! Jeez. I didn't even think of that. What should we do?" What am I, an idiot? Do I live in la-la land so often I can't even remember the hot water heater and the freezer need electricity to work properly? I wonder how many other people are as disconnected as I am?

"Let's go see Bill. He might have a generator we can borrow. After that, we can stop by the grocery store," Aaron says.

It always weirds me out a little when he calls Grandmaster Shane *Bill*. He never does it when we're at the martial arts studio. Like me and the rest of the students, he calls him Master Shane. And Master Shane calls Aaron *Mr. Ogden* and me *Ms. Esplin*. It's an important distinction and a term of respect. He makes a point of reminding the students that, as black belts, we've earned the title. I feel like Master Shane has earned the title off the mat as well. Aaron agrees, but they spend a substantial amount of time together, so it just makes sense for them to use first names.

I nod my agreement as we head slightly out of town to Master Shane's small cabin. Guess our hike for today is called off.

Chapter 9

We pull into Master Shane's house, his dog Freckles baying his greeting. Master steps out on the large front porch and gives us a wave. "Wondered if you'd be stopping by," he says. "Come on up. Freckles, cool it."

Inside the house, he says, "I just started a pot of coffee. Want a cup, Laurie? Aaron, help yourself to a bottle of water."

"You have power?" I ask, looking around the living room. I don't see any artificial light, but the window placement makes for a very bright and airy room.

"Nope. Using a generator as needed, but I made the coffee with my camping pot."

"Sounds great. I'd love a cup." I nod.

Freckles bumps my thigh, looking for some attention. I'm not exactly sure what kind of dog he is, and Master has no idea either. He just calls him a mutt, but he's a sweet thing—definitely some kind of hound, judging by his amazing howling abilities and floppy ears. He's completely adorable.

"You holding up okay, Laurie?" Master Shane asks. "You look tired."

I'm too embarrassed to admit to Master Shane that I was out late partying. I nod and give a weak smile.

"I was wondering if I could borrow your small generator, sir," Aaron says. "My parents have a full freezer, and we didn't even think about it until just a few minutes ago. If we can use the generator, I think I can keep it frozen until they get this mess sorted out. That is, if you think it has enough power to run a freezer?"

"Should be no problem. It's 2200 watts; it powered my camp trailer and will run a fridge. At least, that's what the advertisement for it said. You can borrow it, but I don't have any fuel to send with you."

"My dad has a five-gallon can for the dirt bikes. I can use that."

"Sure, that'll work."

"How often do you think we should run the generator to keep the freezer frozen?" I ask.

"I don't know for sure. I figure an hour or two every day. It's a chest freezer?" We nod and he says, "Keep it closed and it will stay frozen longer. That said, you might want to take out the processed foods and cook those up to eat first. They'll thaw quicker than a big hunk of meat."

"You mean like frozen pizzas and lasagna?"

"Frozen pizza for sure. Lasagna, I don't know. I never buy the stuff."

"Will the generator fit in my car?" I ask.

Aaron says it will, as Master Shane says, "Yeah, no problem. It's just a small one I used in the camp trailer I sold last year."

"Thank you, Master." I say. We only stay long enough for me to finish my coffee. I wouldn't mind visiting and playing with Freckles longer, but Aaron's anxious to leave.

We get the generator set up and plugged into the freezer. Everything seems to go fine. Following Master Shane's suggestion, we cook the pizza, hot pockets, and other things using the grill. We also cook everything in the fridge. We then move the fridge items to the freezer section of the refrigerator, thinking the freezer might stay cooler longer.

"How long do you think the things we cooked will stay good?" Aaron asks. "The last thing we need is food poisoning."

I make a face and shrug. *How would I know?* Cooking and food safety aren't my forte. "We'll feast on the cooked stuff first."

He nods. "I'm going to go to my place and bring over all the food in my fridge and freezer. I think I remember hearing something about a full freezer working better than an empty one, so more can't hurt. And we'll cook up my stuff too. We'll have our meals together while this whole thing is going on."

My breath catches. "Will you be staying over?"

He pauses before saying, "I don't think so. I'll keep the stuff in my cabinets. I can have those for breakfast. I'll come over each evening after work. Maybe we can pack up food for our lunches from whatever we cook that night. We both pack a lunch for work anyway, so that seems easiest. Is that okay?"

"Sure. Easy enough."

"And I'll ride my bike back and forth so we save on fuel. I do it once or twice a week already, so it's not a big deal."

"I can ride my bike to work too." I nod, taking what I assume is a hint.

He responds with a smile. "You still have cash?"

"Around a hundred," I say, thankful my parents have drilled into me the power of money. Even in today's world of debit cards, they've always encouraged me to keep cash on hand. Of course, they'd prefer I keep several hundred in cash. I'm wishing I would've listened to them.

"Let's buy some canned goods and other things we don't need to keep in the fridge."

"We probably should've done that this morning when we were fueling up."

"Right. We should've, but..." He shrugs. "Things feel more urgent than they did this morning."

He's right about that. Aaron takes care of bringing his frozen and refrigerated foods over. As the day goes on, I feel more and more stressed about what's happening.

"Let's get to the grocery store," I say. "We'll take my car."

The radio turns on with the car. *"We're operating on auxiliary power. We'll provide a brief update at the top of each hour."* The radio then goes silent. It's fifteen minutes until the next update.

"I guess I didn't realize they weren't broadcasting all the time." I tell Aaron. "I'd like to wait for the next update, then we can shop."

"Probably a good idea. You want to drive to the store and listen in the parking lot?"

"I guess." I shrug, not really caring.

We don't talk much during our fifteen-minute wait. It's not an uncomfortable silence but not fully companionable either. I don't want to tell him about how I'm concerned the power isn't back on yet. The radio station being on auxiliary power seems to drive this point home.

Chapter 10

"What do you think this means?" I ask Aaron, after listening to the brief update and discovering another terrorist attack has happened. This time, they've taken out oil refineries in the US and even other countries. The station says they're stopping their hourly updates and will remain off the air until 7:00 this evening, when the president is scheduled to speak.

"I'm not entirely sure, but it's not good." He shakes his head. "Not good. Let's make sure we listen to the president when he talks this evening. If they've destroyed so many of the refineries, then we'll definitely have a fuel shortage. So, even when the power comes back on and the freeways are cleared..." This time, his head shake is accompanied by a shrug.

"This is bad. Really bad. Do you think your family will be able to get home?" I ask. "I mean, with a gas shortage, how can they even drive? And if there's a gas shortage, will airplane fuel be a problem too?"

"I don't...I don't know," Aaron takes a deep breath and closes his eyes. "Can I try your phone? See if I can get through to them?"

"Sure, but I don't think it's working." He knows I've tried to call each of our parents several times today, but I don't blame him for wanting to try again.

He tries but it doesn't connect. "How about texting?" I ask.

He nods. "Mind doing it for me? You know I'm all thumbs." I appreciate his attempt at humor.

He tells me what to say, and I send it off. While I have the phone out, I try to log on to the internet. I should've known it'd be a futile effort since the news reminded us the web is offline. They also stressed that all banks and the stock market will be closed for the week.

"Dad will probably make sure they stay at Anna and Hank's house. He'll be keeping up on the news and won't try to make it home until it's okay to do so," Aaron says with a nod. I wonder if he's nodding to convince himself or because he truly thinks this.

"Let's go into the store, get this done," I say.

"Hey, Laurie," a girl who I went to school with, who now works at the grocery store, says as we walk up. "You guys have a flashlight?"

"Hey, Rhonda. I have my phone," I say, pulling it out and activating the flashlight app.

"Good enough. Use this Sharpie to write the price on whatever you buy. The registers can't scan, so this is what we're doing. If you can't find the price on the shelf, ask someone for help. We have a few people roaming around. And it's cash only—well, they'll let you write a check since you two shop here all the time. Just ask Dolly to approve it."

I nod and ask, "Has everything been okay?"

She shrugs. "It's fine. A few people aren't happy we can't take credit cards. Kind of surprising since it's been all over the news about the banks being down, along with credit card and ATM machines." She rolls her eyes.

The grocery store is busy but not crazy. Aaron has about the same amount in cash as me, so we figure that will be more than enough and we won't need to write a check. As we start filling our cart, it's obvious the things I'm comfortable preparing—open a can and heat it up items—have already been purchased. There's a limited selection of things like soup and chili.

I watch as three women, who are somewhere around my age and obviously sisters based on their curly hair and similar features, fill their carts. I catch tidbits of their conversation as they load up with what's available. They sound like they know what they're doing. I follow behind them and mimic their items as best I can, gleaning information as they discuss their food plans.

Aaron adds in items he wants, often reminding me we can cook on the gas stovetop in the house by manually lighting the burner, but we can only do simple baking on the grill since the oven doesn't work without electricity.

As we put the groceries in the car, I can't help but smile. I think we're in pretty good shape. We should have more than enough food to last until the power comes back on and the gas situation gets figured out. I was so scared when we went into the store, after hearing about the refinery explosions and what it could mean for our fuel shortages. But now, just knowing we have food, I think we'll be okay.

Aaron catches my smile and gives me a strange look.

"Sorry, I'm just feeling so...hopeful. So much more now than when we went in. I think we'll be okay with the food at the house and this. Don't you?"

"I'm not sure," Aaron says. "I keep thinking of Mrs. Holland and her 'nine meals to anarchy' thing. Do you think that's real? If it is..." He sighs. "We have food today, but I wonder if someone could try and take it from us tomorrow or the next day. A dad would do anything for his child, and if the child is hungry..." He shakes his head. Aaron definitely knows about the love a dad has for his child.

"Not in Wesley," I say.

"Why not?"

"Because...it's *Wesley*." I gesture to encompass this small town I love. I was born in the hospital in Prospect and lived in Wesley until I went to Laramie for school. Even though I'm a native, my parents made sure we did some traveling during summer vacations. With both of my parents being schoolteachers for most of their careers, we had summers free. And we'd make the most of it. I've been in many other places across the US and even South America, Mexico, and Europe. But Wesley is it for me. It's home and I love it. There's no place like it.

"I don't know, Laurie. I just think people might forget they live in a small town with people they've known forever. I know I'd do just about anything to protect you."

"You wouldn't steal," I say indignantly.

He gives me a long look, then whispers, "I would if I had to."

Chapter 11

Aaron and I take the groceries to my house and put them away. After they're placed in the cabinets and pantry, I'm disappointed to see it's not as much as I thought. With the food already in the house, we'll be fine for several weeks—probably even more than a month—but I truly thought it'd be more. Of course, everything will be fine before then. I'm sure the government is working on these issues and it won't take even close to a month to get everything back to normal.

Aaron checks the water, which is still running, but with less force than usual. We refill the containers I used last night, then he says, "I'm going to run home. I have some empty soda jugs I was going to recycle, but it makes sense to fill them up. With the decrease in pressure, we might lose the tap before much longer."

"You think so?"

He gives me a slightly exasperated look. "I don't *really* know. I just want to be cautious."

"Okay. You'll be back for supper?"

"I will, before then probably. In fact, why don't you come with me? I think...it might..." he stutters, then sighs. "I'd feel better if we were together."

"Go to your place without a chaperone?" I try to keep my voice light and teasing.

His face falls slightly. "It's not like that, Laurie."

"Aaron, you know how I feel about it. At our age—" I purse my lips to help prevent saying something I might regret. Yes, I think his rules are ridiculous at times. I understand why he's so adamant—but seriously?

"You know what? I'll go take care of things and be back in a bit. Make sure you lock the door."

He reaches in to give me a goodbye peck. I don't raise up to meet him, and I make sure to turn my head at the last moment so his kiss lands on my cheek. He gives me a disappointed look.

I hear his key turn the deadbolt, then listen for his truck to start up and drive away. *That man!* He's always so proper. So austere and perfect—prudish even. I should have more of a say in our relationship. He's so...so infuriating.

I feel my blood pounding in my ears. I need a workout to get rid of some of this frustration. I peel off my clothes and put on my dobok, my Taekwondo uniform.

Minutes later I'm in the small workout studio in the basement. I start with some basic stretching, then quickly move to the large, freestanding bag for drills. My first combination is a skipping roundhouse kick with my right leg, then a left counter kick roundhouse. This is a simple combo for getting close and then sliding away, an important skill for sparring—also a great way to start working out my aggression. Shouting at the bag, also called a kihap or kihapping, really helps with my anguish. Nothing like a good yell to release frustration.

After several minutes, I switch to front leg doubles; back-to-back roundhouse kicks alternating the left and right leg. My heart is starting to pound. I suck in a deep breath and switch it up to a right leg roundhouse, then a left side turning back kick.

I finish my bag drill with a series of four body kicks and a head kick, half a dozen sets each leg, focusing on my speed.

I stop for a water break before moving on to Taekwondo forms, called Taegeuk Poomsae. I'm on form two when I hear the door at the top of the stairs open. Aaron. It has to be Aaron. *Right?*

Just in case it's not, I move to a concealed space where I can see whoever is coming down the stairs, but they won't be able to see me unless they know where to look. It's also a good place to launch an attack if needed.

His eyes immediately search out my hiding spot. "You read my mind," Aaron says, already outfitted in his dobok. "Want to spar?"

"Poomsae first," I reply. "You want to stretch?"

He spends several minutes warming up, including some light bag work. I practice kicks, punches, and blocks until he's ready.

We stand side by side facing the mirror. Aaron's a third dan black belt; I'm a second dan. I'll test for third dan next summer. I could've tested for my third dan when Aaron did, but I injured my knee a few months before and wasn't ready. And then I put it off to focus on school.

"Joon bee," he says. *Ready position.*

I move into proper stance, and we start our forms. We work through each until we get to Taebaek, third dan poomsae. I'll have to be super precise on this one for my promotion test. Today, I manage to fumble it.

"Can we do it again?" I ask.

Aaron helps me with it several more times. We practice blocks and kicks before he says, "I know I upset you. I'm sorry, Laurie. And you're right, at our age, we should be able to spend time together—even more time than we do. If I could be sure I wouldn't...I would only...I'm sorry." He hangs his head.

"Aaron, things are different now than they were. Not only are you older, but you know yourself, you know why it's important to you. I know why it's important to you. It's not like I'm going to..." I sigh, thinking of what I want to say. "Aaron, I'm not going to throw myself at you if we happen to be alone. I mean, really, we're alone down here. I don't have a problem with wanting to...to..." I clear my throat and raise my eyebrows.

He gives me a small smile. "We have way too much respect for the mat to even think about *that.*"

The way he says *that* makes me laugh. Not a cute laugh, but a through my nose snort, which makes Aaron snicker, which makes me laugh even harder.

When we get ourselves together, Aaron stares straight ahead, making sure to fully avoid eye contact. "It's just, after Tabitha and how miserable she was, I wouldn't want you to look at me the way she did."

"Aaron Ogden," I say and force him to look at me. "I love you. I loved you like a brother for years. Now I love you as the man you are. Tabitha's unhappiness wasn't because of you. It wasn't your job to make her happy."

I quickly shut my mouth, not wanting to say more.

Aaron and I were good friends for so long. Since I was older, it really was like a brother-sister thing. A few times I wondered if he wanted more; I caught some of the same looks from Aaron that Toby was giving Heather the other night. But I had no idea how serious he was about me until the day he turned eighteen. That day, he came to my house—I was living with my parents then—and said, "Laurie, today is my birthday. I'm eighteen and legal age now. Will you be my girlfriend?"

I was flabbergasted. He was so sweet. He'd dressed up and did something extra to his hair, was even wearing his contacts, which I knew he hated. Part of me really wanted to say yes, but that would've only been to keep from hurting his feelings, which in the end would've hurt his feelings more. I tried to let him down gently. For the next several weeks he was cordial, but our friendship was strained. It wasn't long afterward he started dating Tabitha, or Tabby as she preferred to be called.

Five months later, I was a guest at their wedding. She was just starting to show.

Chapter 12

By the time we're finished, I'm a sweaty, soggy mess. I wish I would've remembered my inability to take a hot shower before embarking on a killer workout.

"How cold do you think the water will be?" I ask Aaron. "Too cold for a quick shower?"

"You could try it. It's probably warmer than swimming in the creek."

"Brrr. I hate swimming in the creek. You know that."

"Well, I'm going to hop in the shower—cold or not. I'll run home and be back shortly."

"Aaron, just use the shower in your parents' room."

He hesitates then nods.

"I'm going to heat some water in a pot so I have a little warm water," I say.

Aaron's gone only a couple of minutes before he returns.

"That was fast."

"Not enough water pressure for the shower to work," he says quietly, calmly.

I'm anything but calm. "What? Does this mean…is the water going to stop working?"

"Maybe; seems it could. I suspect they'll make an announcement when the radio broadcasts again."

"What time did they say," I ask, "7:00?"

"Yeah, when the president speaks."

"You need some of my warm water?"

"Nah. There was enough coming out of the tap to cleanup, just not for an actual shower."

After my pseudo shower, I change into shorts and a T-shirt. Aaron's at the table on the backyard deck writing in a notebook.

"Whatcha doing?"

He pushes his glasses farther up his nose. "Making a list."

"Checking it twice?" I smile.

He gives me his famous half smile. "By the time we're done with it, I think it will be checked way more than twice."

"Oh really?"

"I thought maybe we should do an inventory of all the food and supplies we have."

"For what purpose?"

"I think..." His pause is much longer than it should be—a classic Aaron method for not wanting to say what's on his mind.

"You think..." I prod.

"I think it will be a long time before my parents are able to come home. And not just them, anyone gone now—gone any distance, anyway—and grocery trucks, fuel trucks, any supplies. Mrs. Holland might be right about the anarchy thing too. I think we should make a plan in case things go bad."

"Aaron, *Wesley*, remember? Small town USA. It's not like we're in Detroit or Chicago or someplace dangerous."

"Laurie, *hungry people*, remember?"

I shake my head. There's no use arguing with him. "Show me what you have."

He nods and scoots the notebook so I can see it. "Not much yet. I started with categories. Food is a main category, then I divided that into subcategories. I was going to divide it by food groups, but then thought maybe I should start with perishables and shelf-stable stuff. We need to use up the perishables first. Since I brought all of my fridge and freezer stuff over, too, there's a good amount."

"But if the power comes back on, the freezer and fridge will work again. Besides, we have the generator."

"We do have the generator—and a finite amount of fuel. If the power comes back on, great. But I think we should operate under the assumption it won't be back on any time soon."

"Why would you think that?" I ask, shaking my head. While Aaron's usually a positive person, in the last couple of years, he's become slightly cynical. He used to be more analytical as opposed to pessimistic, which I enjoyed. He'd look at things in such a way that I'd never consider. He still analyzes, but now he over analyzes to the point of negativity in many cases. Oh, I know why he does this now, but it's still annoying.

"These attacks are breaking us down. They've essentially taken out methods of transportation. We're stranded. Wherever anyone is, they have limited options for getting elsewhere. There will be a fuel shortage. I suspect that'll be one thing the president says tonight. Or maybe..."

This time, I wait out his extended pause. I make a concentrated effort not to tap out the Jeopardy ditty on the table as he ponders. Movement at the backyard bird feeder catches my eye. Female house finches, but my dad always calls them tweety birds.

Oh, he knows one bird from the next, even having books on ornithology. But he casually refers to any bird we see frequently as tweety birds—until I correct him. That's part of the game, a way for him to encourage my interest in birdwatching. I smile at the memory.

Could these troubles go on into next year? Is there a chance my parents won't be able to come home when they're supposed to? That doesn't seem at all possible.

Finally, Aaron says, "Or maybe he won't say it. He'll drop hints so we'll know it's bad, but for political reasons, he won't say it outright."

"Political reasons? Who cares about that?" I can hear my voice rising but don't try to control it. "We're in a crisis—more than a crisis."

Aaron shrugs and points at the notebook with his pen. "I broke it down further. Under perishable I have protein, vegetables, and miscellaneous. Under nonperishable I have protein, grains, vegetables, miscellaneous. I have nonfood categories: shelter, self-defense, transportation, cooking supplies, light, first aid supplies, toiletries, and miscellaneous." He looks at me. "Well, what do you think?"

"Very...thorough. But I don't know why you have shelter and transportation. You have an apartment. I have the house. Seems odd to feel the need to list those. And transportation—your truck, my car." I shrug. "Again, why list them?"

"True. And those things will all go on the list," he says as he starts writing. "Okay, so should we continue with shelter? My place, your place, and I think we should add the martial arts studio. We can go there if we have to. Bill's place also."

"Why the studio and Master Shane's?"

"In case we couldn't stay here or at my apartment."

"We?"

"In case something happened to my place, I'd stay here. If something happened here, you could stay at my apartment."

Really? I hide a smile. "Something like what?"

46

"You know how we heard about fires breaking out in different places? Remember the college town that pretty much burned to the ground? Same thing could happen here. And now, with the water pressure gone, how would our fire department put the fire out?"

"Okay. Good point," I agree.

"I have my backpacking gear, which includes a small one-person tent. I'm going to go through my family's stuff and put a pack together for you. They have a variety of tents, tarps, and other things."

"All right."

He flips to the transportation page, writing down his pickup and my car. "We have the mountain bike, my dirt bike, plus my family's dirt bikes and bicycles. Oh, and the trailer for hauling the bikes. If it was winter, we'd have snowshoes and cross-country skis as additional options. You think those should go on the list?"

"It's June, Aaron."

"It is." He nods.

"What's that look?" I ask, trying to read his face.

Very quietly, only slightly above a whisper, he says, "I'm scared, Laurie."

Chapter 13

Aaron and I work on the list. Part of me thinks we're majorly overreacting. Then I think of the lady from church and her nine meals to anarchy. That, combined with Aaron's fervent belief a dad will do anything if his child is hungry—maybe we're not overreacting?

We enter things we know off the top of our head first, deciding we'll start rummaging around the house and detail the items tomorrow evening after work. We're pretty much done with our first draft when it's time to listen to the president's talk. Aaron brings out the battery-operated radio his younger brother Micah uses. We find the station, and at precisely 7:00, without any music or fanfare, the president begins his address.

"Good evening. I'm speaking to you tonight to give you a report on the situation our country is facing. The loss of life over the past several days has been staggering. My prayers and condolences go out to all who have lost loved ones.

"I regret to say, the assaults upon our nation continue, with the latest attacks on our oil refineries today at 10:22 am eastern time.

"Today's incidents further complicate our already vulnerable position. Friday's attacks on our cities' bridges caused a mass exodus from the affected cities as our citizens tried to find a place they could feel safe. The small towns and communities of which our people fled to have had a very difficult time accommodating the abundance of new inhabitants. Resources were rapidly depleted. We enacted a program to send aid to the areas in most dire need.

"The cyberwar, which began yesterday, complicated this aid when the bulk of our nation's power grids were taken offline. One of our main goals was supplying fuel to these areas so people could return to their homes. The lack of electricity impeded this process. The destruction of more than half of our US refineries, and several refineries in other countries, means we now face a certain worldwide shortage of fuel."

I start crying. Aaron puts his arm around me, and I rest my head on his shoulder. Any hope I felt earlier today has been crushed. Aaron hands me a tissue and grabs one for himself.

"We will bring our unaffected refineries to their full capabilities, and we will rebuild our destroyed refineries.

"Our financial institutions have been impaired by the cyberwar. Because of continued attacks on our systems, we were left no choice but to take the internet offline. This prevents the use of credit cards through the online network. ATMs are also unavailable. As a result of all financial records relying on internet access, I've declared a banking holiday, beginning tomorrow and continuing through this week.

"The American Stock Exchange, the Nasdaq Stock Market, and the New York Stock Exchange, after consultation with the US Securities and Exchange Commission, and in light of the outrageous attacks on America and continued cyberattacks, will also be closed for the week. Our hope is we can stop the cyberwar and remedy any damage caused within this time.

"The cyberwar has taken almost every power station offline, either fully or partially. For most people, this power outage is simply an inconvenience, not a tragedy. We're providing as much help as we can to healthcare facilities that require power to operate. Backup systems are in place and believed to be functioning.

"Do remember, with summer temperatures and the lack of air conditioning, you want to do what you can to keep yourself cool. My experts tell me a wet T-shirt can help lower your core temperature. You can also use small, manual, handheld fans to provide additional relief. The very young and the elderly are most susceptible to heat exhaustion. These people who are most likely to be affected will need extra care and monitoring.

"While it seems we're in dire straits, I assure you, the functions of our government continue without interruption. We're working to get help to those who have been injured, and we're taking precautions to protect our citizens from further attacks.

"The search is underway to find those who have carried out these malicious attacks. Once located, they will be dealt with and brought to justice.

"Within our borders, we're experiencing many instances of violence in our cities, including riots, looting, arson, and other criminal activities. In the areas which have been hardest hit, the

National Guard is being brought in based on requests from individual governors.

"I ask the help of every person—whether in the cities, small towns, or rural areas—to band together during this distressing time. It will take all of us working with one goal in mind to come through this time intact. The goal of preserving our great nation and citizens. The goal of preventing riots and destruction. The goal of not just 'getting through' this travesty but of enduring and becoming a much stronger nation because of it. We will never forget. We will move forward and come together as one nation, indivisible.

"Thank you. Good night. God bless the United States of America."

There's a loud screech, then the radio announcer comes on.

"We'll replay tonight's presidential address in its entirety at 8:00 pm tonight and tomorrow at 7:00 am and 1:00 pm.

"Now, for local news, we have reports of scattered burglaries and looting in various businesses throughout our county and surrounding area. We have been asked to pass on the request from local police to remain in your homes from dusk to dawn. While a curfew is not officially in effect, anyone on the streets during nondaylight hours will be deemed to have nefarious intentions and will be stopped, with arrest likely. This request remains in effect for the duration of this crisis.

"Please remember to continue to boil or otherwise purify all water from public sources or to use only bottled water. We do not believe the water supply in our area was affected by the terrorists but know this could change. If you're unable to purify water at home due to the power outage, you can obtain purified water at City Park in Wesley and Pryor, Prospect Chamber of Commerce, and the Rendezvous Museum parking lot in Rendezvous. We're receiving scattered reports saying the municipal water supply is failing in some areas. If your tap water stops working, you can go to the previously listed places for a daily supply of water.

"We're still operating on backup power. To conserve this power, we'll drop our broadcasts to 7:00 am, 1:00 pm, and 7:00 pm beginning tomorrow. We'll also broadcast any time there's an urgent alert via the Emergency Alert System. Our sister station, KWDI at 870 AM, will broadcast at 5:00 am and 5:00 pm, in addition to any EAS broadcasts. We welcome donations of diesel fuel to use in our generators at either of our station locations. Thank you and good night."

"It definitely doesn't sound good," I say, after blowing my nose. "You were right to start the list. And," I take a deep breath, "I think we'll need snowshoes and skis added to the transportation list. It doesn't sound like things are going to be back to normal any time soon. You think your mom's boots will fit me? Gosh, Aaron, I need winter clothes. I left everything in the storage unit I rented in Laramie. That seemed smarter than hauling things I wouldn't need for the summer back and forth. But now..." I start to cry again.

"Mom's and Elizabeth's things will fit you," he says, once again pulling me close. "They'll be in the same situation in Wisconsin. They only have what's in their suitcases."

Aaron lets me cry for several more minutes, then suggests we spend a little more time working on our list. Finally, he says, "I'll be over after work tomorrow. We'll start on the pantry and start organizing things. I was thinking the items we deem essential could all be put together. And maybe, if we have duplicates of things, we should keep some at my apartment—food too. We'll stick with keeping the cold stuff here because of the generator. But we can split the pantry food, that way we don't lose all of it if something happens to one of our places."

"It's a good idea," I agree. "I'll be home from work before you get off, so I'll start with the pantry."

Aaron pulls me tight, holding me closer than he usually allows—and for longer. When I lift up for a kiss, he delivers—and not his usual chaste peck.

"I love you. I know some of my...rules drive you crazy. But I promise you, it isn't for lack of love. I've loved you for so long, Laurie. I just couldn't bear anything happening to you."

"Aaron," I say softly, "I've said this many times, but I'll say it again. I'm not Tabitha. I love you, for you. Not because I'm being forced to or I'm expected to. Not for any reason other than because of you. I love you with...with a passion a woman has for her man, for her husband to be. I'll continue to follow your rules." I waggle my eyebrows at him, which prompts a sideways grin. "But when we're married...you'd better watch out, buster."

Aaron throws back his head and laughs. "You're a goofball, Laurie." With that, he gives me another kiss—his usual peck this time—and steps out the door, saying, "Keep it locked."

After Aaron leaves, I wander around for a few minutes, thinking of the president's talk and our list. Soon, I'm in tears again. Instead of fighting them, I allow myself a good cry.

The sun has yet to set when I decide I might as well go to bed. After being out late at last night's bonfire—and over imbibing—along with the stress of the day, bed sounds like the best place.

I have a momentary pang of sadness, or maybe it's longing, wishing Aaron could be here. Oh, not longing exactly for the obvious reason of him sleeping over, but for the closeness, the togetherness, especially because I'm feeling so worn out and vulnerable. And scared. For him to admit his fear earlier, it drives home just how serious things are.

Would a dad do anything to feed his child? Could one of the neighbors decide to break in and take our food? I think of Rolly Reynolds up the street. He and his wife have two children, one born only days before Mr. and Mrs. Ogden left for Wisconsin, the other a toddler. Would Rolly break in here and take what he wanted? What if he felt they'd need it to survive? Aaron would know how deep that parental love goes.

I sat in the back row at Aaron and Tabitha's wedding. There were around a hundred guests, and not many looked like they wanted to be there.

Especially Tabitha.

I've never seen such an unhappy bride. Even though Tabitha didn't have the glow of an enthusiastic bride, the wedding was quite an elaborate affair. The engagement was only about a month, but Tabby's parents spared no expense or extravagance.

As a real estate agent in nearby Prospect and a deacon at our former church, her dad made it very clear there would be a wedding and it would be suitable, even if it was under unsavory conditions. Tabitha's mom wasn't nearly as enthusiastic and had suggested Tabitha go live with relatives, give up the baby, and then get on with her life.

Of course, I didn't know any of this when I received the wedding invitation or as I was sitting in the audience. Aaron's sister Elizabeth shared all the gossipy details later, after…after it all happened.

Even though Tabby was not an enthusiastic bride, Aaron was smiling and happy. I watched as he gasped, joy and love filling his face, when she entered the room. Her formal white gown with a long train and veil were very becoming. But the scowl on her face ruined the illusion.

As I'm washing my face in preparation for bed, the music starts. *Another street party?* I peer out the bedroom window, looking toward the end of the cul-de-sac where last night's bonfire was. No fire, no people in the street.

I turn my head, trying to determine which direction the music is originating from.

I give up after a minute or so and finish getting ready for bed. As tired as I am, maybe the music won't bother me.

I'm almost asleep, the *boom, boom, boom* of the base acting as a lullaby, when the shouting starts.

Chapter 14

I bolt upright in bed. Another scream—I scoot to the window, peering out. There's a group of people circled up on Heather's lawn, but it's too dark for me to make out who's in the group. As I watch, many of them step back. Then I notice someone lying on the ground. One of the others—a man, judging by the size of him—is standing over the person on the ground. I gasp as he draws back his leg and kicks.

Someone screams again, a female this time. *Heather?* Whatever is going on out there, it's not okay. I grab my robe and shove my feet into my slippers before running down the stairs and out the door. I'm advancing on the group at a run. It's Heather along with another girl—both are screaming, saying, "Stop, don't hurt him," or something similar.

Without anyone seeming to notice me, I skid to a stop as I reach the lawn. Heather and a girl around her age are both crying, begging the kicker to stop. There are five more guys standing around, their backs all to me. Based on their sizes, all seem to be full-grown men. I suddenly think about how stupid I am for being here. I'm completely unarmed, wearing a robe and slippers with jammies underneath.

Why didn't I at least think to bring the handgun? Or the shotgun? That would've been better. I could slide the rack and they'd know I mean business. I should just go for help. The city police station isn't far. Yes, that's what I'll do.

"Laurie!" Heather yells before I can turn tail and run.

The guy kicking the figure on the ground stops. Heather and the other girl rush to the crumpled form. The kicker turns to me and casually says, "Oh, hey. Sorry for the disturbance. We were just having a little..." he pauses, then says, "attitude adjustment."

I watch as Heather rolls the human lump over. "Toby," I gasp. "You-you people should be ashamed of yourselves for beating up this child."

"He's fine," a deep voice booms. I turn to see Chuck from the bonfire, the guy who helped me get my way-too-strong drinks.

"He's a child." I step toward Toby. "This is done. Go away," I say with as much force as I can muster.

"Yep, sure," says the kicker. "I think maybe we made our point. This child," he jerks his thumb in Toby's direction, "can't be disrespecting me or my friends. Got it, *Laurie*?" he sneers.

"Let's go, Jeremy," Chuck says.

He nods. "Okay, man. Heather, Cheyenne, we'll see you two later."

"No. Don't," Heather says. "I don't want to see you. Don't come back here."

"Whatever, sweetheart," Jeremy says, as he and his posse walk away.

Chuck turns back and says, "See *you* later, Laurie." The way he says it causes a shudder to run through me. Last night he seemed nice enough. Tonight, he's a definite creeper.

I rush to Toby. Through gritted teeth, he says, "I'm okay. They weren't really trying to hurt me, not too bad anyway."

He might think that, but the blood on his face and his difficulty with not only talking but breathing say otherwise. *Are they really gone?* I look around. Seems so.

"You need a doctor," I say. "Heather and..."

"Cheyenne," the other girl says.

"Right. Stay with him and keep an eye out for those guys. I'm getting my car, and we're taking him to the clinic."

Heather wipes her nose on her shirttail. "Hurry, Laurie."

Chapter 15

"Go faster," Heather screeches. "He's…passed out or something."

"Is he still breathing?" I ask, holding my breath.

Cheyenne, sitting in the front passenger seat, twists around and yells, much too loudly for the space we're in, "Heather? Is he breathing?"

"Jeez, Cheyenne, thanks for blowing out my eardrums. Yeah, he's breathing. Just not awake."

We practically skid into the clinic parking lot. Before the car comes to a complete stop, I yell for Cheyenne to run inside and get some help. This isn't a hospital, per se; it's really more of a triage center. They have a couple of nurses and a doctor available, and also an ambulance on call. For anything serious, they transport to the full-service hospital in Prospect.

I open the back door.

"His breathing sounds terrible," Heather says. "It's all rattled. I think he's really hurt."

"They'll take care of him," I say, as Cheyenne runs out with a vaguely familiar woman wearing scrubs.

"He was beat up?" the woman asks.

"Yes," Heather cries. "They hit him and then pushed him to the ground, and one kept kicking him."

"All right. Thad is right behind me with a gurney. We'll evaluate him and see what needs to happen next. Where are his parents?"

"They—" Heather breaks down in tears.

"Denver." I say, "They were on a weekend trip with her parents." I gesture toward Heather. "They're stuck there for now."

She nods with understanding. "How old is he?"

"Seventeen," Heather whispers between her tears.

Thad appears with the gurney. Within a few minutes, Toby's inside. With Heather's help, I complete the essential paperwork.

About ten minutes later, another nurse—a girl from school, who's a couple of years older than I am, who's name escapes me—comes out and says, "We're going to transport him to Prospect. With the fuel shortage, we're trying to treat as many people in-house as we can, but he needs more care than we're equipped to provide. Do you have any gas you can contribute to get him there?"

I think about the fuel for the generator. It's not much, and we need it for the freezer, but Toby's life could depend on him getting to the Prospect hospital. I'm about to offer it, when Heather says, "I can get gas. Laurie, can you take me home? We'll be right back."

"Okay," the nurse says. "We'll have him ready to go within fifteen minutes."

I peer at her nametag. "Thank you, Jane. We'll be back."

"I'm going too," Cheyenne says. "I just want to go home."

We drop Cheyenne off at her house and then go to Heather's. I consider stopping at my place to change out of my robe and pajamas, but I don't want to take the time. Heather has a five-gallon and a two-gallon fuel can. She holds them between her feet in the front seat. We drive with the windows down, and the fumes are still overwhelming. I try to ignore just how unsafe we're being.

When we return to the clinic, they're ready to put Toby in the ambulance. "How will we find out about him?" Heather asks.

"We have a working radio we're using to communicate with Prospect and other hospitals," Jane says. "I already called the sheriff about this, so they'll probably stop by your homes for a statement. No one was available at the moment to come here."

"We'll have to talk to the police?" Heather asks.

Jane shrugs. "Probably. You can come back tomorrow after 2:00 pm. We'll get an update on him shortly before then. And when he's ready to be discharged, you'll have to make arrangements to get him."

"Okay, sure," I say.

We wait until Toby is gone, then I turn to Heather and say, "Maybe you should stay with me tonight. Just in case those guys come back."

She chews on her thumbnail a moment before shaking her head. "I'll be fine."

"You sure? Tonight has been rather traumatic. I know I'm a mess and wouldn't mind your company."

Heather nods. "I'm sure. I just want to go to bed. Besides, they won't bother me. They were just mad at Toby." She goes back to working on her thumbnail, then says, "It wasn't so much they were mad at him. More like Jeremy thought he was being disrespectful."

"In what way?" I ask. She shrugs her response and rips off the last bit of nail.

After dropping Heather off, I start warming some water so I can wash away Toby's blood. I totally lose control and start bawling. I don't even bother to try to contain myself until the teakettle whistles.

I doze a little but mostly toss and turn for what little remains of the night. Finally, as the sun starts to rise, I give up any attempts at sleep and get ready for work.

I make a rather large breakfast of scrambled eggs, precooked sausage links, and bread—not toast since the toaster isn't working with the power out. And more of the instant coffee. Aaron said I could boil water and add coffee grounds, then strain the grounds out. It's his dad's preferred way for having coffee on the trail. But for today, I'm still taking the easy route with the instant coffee. My breakfast tastes like sawdust. I end up making a sandwich out of it and choking it down.

I'm ready in plenty of time to ride my bike to work. In fact, I'll be early. That's fine; it's better than sitting around here. When I arrive at work, there's a sign on the front door. *Closed Until Crisis Is Over.*

I sigh. I should've realized this. With the power out and the fuel shortage, of course Dr. Anderson would close. It only makes sense. Well, I guess I'll have plenty of time to work on the inventory list today. I told Heather I'd stop by the clinic when I get off at 3:00 to see how Toby is doing. I'll make a point of going at 2:00 when they said they'd have news. I start to ride back home and decide to take a detour by Aaron's work. Will they still be open with all of the troubles? I guess, since Aaron's in charge while his boss is gone, that will be his call.

The main bay of the garage is open, so I ride over to it. Aaron's sitting in a chair, staring off into space. "Hey," I say.

He jumps. "Laurie! What are you doing?"

I can't help but laugh. "Scaring you, apparently."

He gives me a small smile.

"You were deep in thought," I say.

"I was. I was trying to decide if I should close up for the day...well, for several days."

"Dr. Anderson is closed," I say, then go on to tell him about the sign on the door. "And..." I hesitate while I think of how I want to word my next statement.

"And?"

58

"And I need to tell you about what happened last night." I give him the details of the attack on Toby, trying to downplay just how scared I was and how I may have been in danger when I went running out like a fool.

When I'm done, I can tell he's not happy. Instead of telling me how unhappy he is, he says, "I think I'll close up. I'm the only one who came in to work anyway. With the bay door open, there's enough light I can work, but it will be much slower without the air compressor, and I need electricity for that."

He shrugs. "But really, who's going to come around for car work with everything going on? And how will they pay? Almost everyone pays with credit card, which we can't take. So..."

He stares at the car in front of him. "I finished this one. There's another one I can work on that came in last week, but it'd be a chore with manual tools. I'm going to wait on it—wait until this is over. I think I'll put up a sign like Dr. Anderson did. Maybe even make it so people can leave me notes. I can drop by and check it each day."

"In case someone has a car emergency?"

Aaron gives me a stern look. "I'm trying hard not to be upset with you. I know you did what you thought you should do, but..." He physically bites his lip to prevent whatever it was he planned on saying next. Aaron has never had much of a temper. As long as I've known him, he's always been easy going, not letting much bother him. I saw him angry once at a Taekwondo tournament, when a guy took a cheap shot. The look on his face was similar to the look he just gave me. The guy was disqualified and Aaron won the bout.

The guy was a poor loser and attacked Aaron in the hallway when he was going for a snack. Then it wasn't just a look on his face, Aaron fully defended himself—no holds barred. And he was angry. Unlike anything I would've expected from the sweet, calm, quiet Aaron I'd known for years. And I've heard from Aaron there was one other time he lost his temper in a similar manner. The night Tabitha—

"So, let me make the sign, and I'll ride home with you," he says, putting on a false smile. "We can get going on our list."

Chapter 16

We ride our bikes to my house in silence. Once there, almost immediately we begin organizing—taking inventory. Aaron's quiet, speaking in a monotone voice, only giving me the information I need to add to the list. After an hour of what I've determined is the silent treatment, I've had enough.

He's kneeling in the pantry, reading me items from the bottom shelf as I list them. I throw the notebook on the counter, then turn to him, hands on my hips. "Look, I know you're mad at me, but you're just going to have to get over it. While running out there may have been stupid, I'd do it again. I'm not going to sit idly by and watch someone get the tar beat out of them."

"I know," he says quietly. "I know you did what you had to do. But you need to think about yourself. You could've been hurt. Killed." He blinks rapidly.

My anger dissolves instantly. "It was stupid. I should've at least taken one of the guns. I just didn't think…I'm not used to having a gun around."

"I know. And because of that, I think we should stop with the list and take you shooting."

"I know how to shoot, Aaron," I say indignantly.

"You do, but you could use more practice."

Master Shane lives on forty acres outside of Wesley. He has a small outdoor shooting range we've used many times; Master Shane has given Aaron an open invitation for its use. We take my car. Master Shane isn't home when we get there, but we set up and use the range anyway.

We spend a couple of hours practicing. Most of the time, I'm dry firing the pistol so I can get comfortable with it. Aaron brought a couple of holsters so I can get used to carrying it on my hip and drawing. Even with the gun unloaded, I'm nervous and awkward. Shooting is fine; it's the taking it in and out of the holster that trips me up. I mainly practice with a 9-millimeter. Aaron says it's the gun his dad taught him and his younger siblings to shoot with. He also has me shoot a few other handguns; one is a revolver, and the other two are different semi-automatics.

By the time we're done, I'm tired. My back hurts, and my lack of sleep last night is catching up with me.

"You did well," Aaron says, handing me my water bottle.

"You think?"

"Yeah. I know the holster is hard for you, but by the end, it was much better. And you really have the shotgun down, no problem. Even shooting it from the hip seemed smooth."

"I only live fired twice today."

"Still, all of the practicing is good. You'll develop muscle memory."

I shrug as I climb in the car. "What time is it?"

"About 2:00," he says. "Let's head over to the clinic and get an update on Toby."

Toby is doing well but needs to stay at least another day. We're supposed to stop by tomorrow to find out if he's ready to be discharged. We're reminded we'll need to go and pick him up. I stop by Heather's house to give her the news, but she's not home, so I leave a note on the door.

We work on our inventory for a couple more hours. Aaron puts together not one but two nice backpacks for me full of all sorts of camping gear, then builds a second one for himself. He wasn't kidding about his family having all kinds of camping and backpacking stuff.

Afterwards, we get ready to go to our Monday night Taekwondo practice. When we arrive at the studio to set up for our 5:30 practice, the windows are boarded up and there's a note on the door—similar to Dr. Anderson's note—*Closed until the power is back.*

"I'm surprised Master Shane would close the dojang," I say.

"Yeah," Aaron agrees. "He must…" He shakes his head, then says, "I'm surprised too."

"You want to go inside? We can still work out."

"It'd be too dark with the windows boarded over. But I do want to grab something from my locker. Want to come with me?" He's already unlocking the door and flips his keychain flashlight on.

"Can I just wait here?"

"Sure. Be right back."

I sit down at a picnic bench in front of the building. We often have Saturday workshops and take our lunches here. My parents were amazing about helping me pursue martial arts. I know at times it was

61

a struggle for them to pay for everything. Not only do the lessons cost money, but there are additional costs for uniforms, clinics, tournaments, and a charge every time I advanced a belt. We weren't a wealthy family; we weren't destitute but didn't have a lot of excess money.

My mom stayed home with me until I went to school. That first year, she was a teacher's aide, or what they call a para. The next year, she taught kindergarten and stuck with that for her career. It was nice having the same schedule as her. She'd take me to school and pick me up afterward. Other than Aaron, my mom has always been my best friend.

Oh, not the "I can get away with whatever I want" best friend. No way. She was strict, and I was expected to behave. And believe me, when I was younger, I didn't want to admit she was my friend. But now, at the ripe old age of twenty-five, I know she is.

When will I see her again? When will they be able to come home? Spending this time on a mission in India has been a dream come true for them. They'd been financially supporting the widow's foundation since I turned fifteen. That year, we all three made a commitment to dine out one time less each month. That money was our offering to the church in India. Two years ago, the year before my dad retired from his high school teaching job, they started talking about going to India.

At first, I thought they were joking. But soon, everything was arranged and our church was holding fundraisers to get them there. My mom is ten years younger than my dad and took early retirement.

The church still supports them financially so they can stay there. But now…what will happen? They're supposed to come home next summer. Surely everything will be back to normal by then, but how can we send them money to help them live?

"I'm finished," Aaron says, startling me from my thoughts. "Let's go to my place. I want to grab my truck and start taking half the stuff over to my apartment like we talked about."

As agreed, he takes about half of the pantry items, first aid stuff, clothes, and one of my new filled-to-the-gills backpacks. Aaron leaves the second backpack he made for himself at my house.

After we're done, Aaron and I go back to organizing his parents' house while we wait. Like before, there's no fanfare when at exactly 7:30 the president starts.

"Ladies and gentlemen, I come to you tonight to share additional heartbreak. The attacks on our country continue. At approximately 6:30 pm eastern, a series of explosions affected our nation's railway system. Railroad bridges were destroyed, tracks were mangled, and tunnels were collapsed. There were many derailments. Commuter, passenger, and freight lines were all afflicted. At this time, due to continued communication issues, we do not have a complete accounting of the destruction. My prayers continue to be with all affected by these acts of terrorism."

He's quiet for several seconds. I look to Aaron, who answers me with a shrug. There's a deep breath, then the president starts again.

"Around the time we received the first reports of the railroad catastrophe, I was privately notified of the loss of several members of Congress in separate events.

"My fellow Americans, your legislators were targeted. They were murdered in cold blood. At this moment, we can confirm the loss of 28 senators and 142 representatives. We're working hard to make contact with every member of Congress so we can help protect the remaining members.

"My wife and I are deeply pained by the losses, which began on Thursday evening and continue through today. We believe we share this pain with all in our great country and even around the world. These losses are something we will carry with us through all of our days. The tens of thousands of Americans who have lost their lives will never be forgotten. Our senators and representatives will never be forgotten.

"We continue to search for those responsible for these atrocities committed on our soil and to our citizens. We will leave no stone unturned in our search for justice. And as you hear my words today, you can be assured we will find justice.

"During this difficult time, we must remember to be united as Americans. We shouldn't be fighting and trying to destroy each other. Save your anger for the enemy, not your neighbor, not your fellow American. The looting and vandalism must come to an end. We're working tirelessly to provide needed assistance to the areas which have been hardest hit by the travesties of the last several days.

"None of us will forget these trying times. We will go forward into a new world—a world where we can once again live in security and freedom.

"Thank you. Good night and God bless America."

Aaron has his arm around me, and I'm crying—again. I glance toward him. He's not teary eyed; he's mad. He catches my eye and says, "I can't believe they'd do that. Why assassinate our legislators? What do they gain by that?"

I shrug my answer as I wipe at my eyes.

He continues, "Fear. They did it to instill fear."

"With everything else happening, isn't there enough fear?" I ask.

"There is. But now they're showing us no one is safe. They got to all of those people, people who were public figures."

We sit quietly for many minutes before Aaron asks, "Are you ready to call it a day?"

Chapter 17

On a normal day off of work, I'd lounge in bed, linger over coffee, play on my phone, and take my time getting dressed. There's nothing normal about this Tuesday off work.

I'm up with the sun, fully dressed, including my athletic shoes. Aaron will be here soon so we can continue our organizing.

I get the coffee water ready; I'll start it to boil after Aaron arrives. Not instant this morning, instead he's making his dad's camping coffee. I can hardly wait...seriously, the idea of brewed coffee of any sort is terribly exciting.

The first time I had coffee was with my dad. I'd often beg a sip off of him. Eventually, he started making me my own cup. Not a cup of coffee really, but warm milk with a dash of coffee, just enough to slightly change the color. The coffee was wonderful, but mostly I loved that Dad would make it special for me.

I still prefer my coffee with cream, but even before the power went out, I usually drank it black. I started drinking it black when I went off to college. It was easier than trying to keep my roommates out of my cream.

This morning's breakfast will look the same as what I ate yesterday; the last three eggs, the last four pieces of bread, and the sausage links we precooked. The generator is working fine for keeping things cold, but I'm starting to worry about the gas. If things are as bad as they sound, we won't be able to find additional fuel to keep the generator going. Then what?

Maybe Heather has more fuel? Or maybe there's some at Toby's house. We'll have to take one of our cars to go and get him from the hospital. We're going to the clinic this afternoon to find out when he'll be discharged. Surely, if he has fuel, he'll reimburse us for what we use.

If we syphon from the cars, we can use it for the generator. Do I have any idea how to syphon? No...but I'm sure Aaron does. He knows all that kind of stuff.

It's about 7:30 when Aaron arrives. After the perfunctory hello kiss, he says, "You want to go for a jog before breakfast?"

I make a face.

He laughs. "I know it's not your favorite. But we should keep up with our physical fitness."

"You jog. I'll stick with working out in the basement and riding my bike everywhere."

He gives me a disappointed look. "Fair enough. I'm going to jog from here to the river trail. I'll be back within half an hour."

"Are you going to jog in your blue jeans," I ask, motioning to his current attire.

He smiles. "Nope. I brought my gym bag. I'll change and then take off. By the way, have you checked the water this morning?"

"No. I washed my face and brushed my teeth with the jug of boiled water I have in the bathroom. I didn't turn on the faucet."

"It was barely a trickle at my house," he says, while walking toward the kitchen. "I was able to get enough to fill and boil about three gallons last night. Darn. It's even slower here." He lets out a big sigh and shakes his head. "Well, we have some stored. We'll be fine for a few days. At least the toilet will still work."

"You think there will be enough water to refill the toilet? How?"

"Sorry, not what I meant. The homes in this neighborhood are still on septic tanks. While they have city water, they haven't hooked into city sewer. I think there's a chance, if the water stops working, the sewer system will also stop."

I make a face, thinking about people in Wesley not being able to flush their toilets. "Ewww...that doesn't sound good."

Aaron nods. "You shouldn't have any trouble with flushing. You'll need to fill the bowl with water, but it should work. Maybe only flush if you have to."

"What about you? Your place doesn't have a septic tank."

"Right. I don't know. Maybe I'm wrong and I can still flush the toilet if I put water in the bowl."

"Will your neighbors know they can do that?"

"They should. I'll talk with a few of them. We'll need more water. Maybe we can get some from Bill. He's on a well, so...."

"So he'll have water as long as his generator is working?" I ask.

Aaron nods. "Should. I'm going to get going. Be back in a bit."

"Okay. I'll start emptying out your mom's bathroom. She keeps their medicine and stuff in there. I'll get the coffee water going and start breakfast so it's ready when you get back. Don't be late. I'm jonesing for coffee." I give him a wink

Aaron takes off, and I start with emptying everything from the master bathroom, spreading the goods out on the dining room table for inventorying and dividing. I think we're a little ridiculous for sharing things between the two houses. Aaron's reasoning makes sense on why, but really?

I can't help but believe Wesley, and our entire Prospector County, won't have the issues we were hearing about in other places, before the TV went out and our twenty-four-hour news cycle ceased to exist.

I have my arms full of towels when Aaron returns after only about ten minutes.

"Change your mind?" I ask.

"Um, yes, sort of."

I sit the towels on the table and turn to fully look at him. He's pale and shaking.

"Aaron? What's going on?"

"I don't..." He shakes his head. "It's okay. I just had a...had a run–in."

"A run–in? What does that mean?"

"There were...there are people camping on the river."

"Camping? Why?"

"I don't know why. I didn't ask them. Didn't really think much about it. Saw them, figured I'd take a wide berth. But one of them..." Aaron takes a deep breath and blurts, "He shot at me."

"Shot at you!" I rush toward him. "Are you okay? I don't see any blood."

"No, no blood. I'm okay. He hit the tree next to me. A splinter hit me, but I'm fine."

"Let me see."

"Nothing to see. It didn't even leave a mark. I'm fine."

I nod. "We need to go to the police."

"Yes, definitely. I'll change and we'll go."

Chapter 18

Fifteen minutes later, we're pulling into the Wesley Police Department parking lot.

"I've never seen so few people here," I say.

"Yeah." Aaron nods. "Pretty dead."

When we get to the door, we discover why. Like Dr. Anderson's clinic, Aaron's shop, and our martial arts studio, the police station is closed. This sign indicates we can go to the county sheriff substation on C Street if we have an emergency.

"This is definitely an emergency," I say needlessly.

Aaron gives his thoughtful look where he scrunches his nose, which raises his glasses. "It's a dangerous situation for sure. What if some kid went on the trail?"

The substation has several more cars, and the door is wide open. I let out a breath I didn't know I was holding. I guess part of me thought the sheriff's department might have pulled out also. Inside, several people are sitting in chairs, filling out papers or talking. There's a small line at the desk. We wait several minutes for our turn.

Stepping forward, I give a courtesy greeting to the lady at the desk. "Hello, Mrs. Daniels."

"Well, Laurie Esplin," she smirks, "I was thinking about your mom yesterday. You must be a wreck."

Her obvious pleasure at my being a wreck does nothing to stop my tears. I blink rapidly to shoo them away. To keep from being a continual wreck, I try *not* to think of my mom and dad. "I'm, uh, yeah. But at least we don't think anything is happening in India, so they should be okay."

"Well, I guess that's something," she says, flicking her hand dismissively. "Now, what can I do for you?" She directs her attention at me only, refusing to even glance in Aaron's direction.

Monica Daniels is a member of the church we all used to belong to. At one point, my mom and her were pretty good friends. Then, when everything happened with Aaron and Tabitha, their friendship kind of fell apart. Seems Mrs. Daniels is a terrible gossip, and my mom told her she didn't want to hear about it. That didn't sit well with Mrs.

Daniels. She even started spreading some minor rumors about my parents in her effort to retaliate against my mom. Yeah, Monica Daniels is not my favorite person.

Aaron knows about the rumors of him and Tabitha...well, really, just about him. Always gracious Aaron says, "Hello, Mrs. Daniels."

She scowls and motions for him to get on with it.

He nods. "Are you working with the county sheriff now?"

"We've joined forces," she says with a huff. "While many of you civilians can just close up shop and stay home, those of us in public service have to figure out a way to keep things running. There isn't enough natural light in the city building. The substation is slightly better."

"Very smart," Aaron says. "I know we all appreciate your dedication."

Mrs. Daniels sits a little straighter. Something resembling a smile crosses her face. "Yes, well, thank you. We get so little appreciation for the things we're doing, you know." She softens her tone slightly. "Now, what is it you need?"

"I found a camp by the river this morning. One of the campers took a shot at me."

A look of shock crosses her face, but she quickly masks it. "Did you provoke them?"

I'm sure I now have my own look of shock. *What a snot she is.*

Aaron shakes his head. "No ma'am."

"Oh, well, okay then. We should have you talk with someone. Unfortunately, I'm the only one here right now. You can fill out a form, and someone will stop by later if they need more information."

"Will you call one of the deputies on the radio?" Aaron asks.

She gives him a dirty look and snaps, "The deputies and officers are all busy. There's an incident happening in Prospect that's of vital importance. They'll get to your problem when they're available."

I start to give her a piece of my mind, but Aaron touches my arm and calmly says, "Thanks so much, Mrs. Daniels. I'm sure you'll give this the proper attention needed. While I wasn't hurt when the guy shot at *me*, I'd sure hate for someone else to wander in that direction and..." He lets his voice fade off, before he says, "At least I'll have a clear conscience and be able to say, 'I know Mrs. Daniels is on it. She'll take care of it.'"

The look she gives him could melt ice. "You can rest assured, Aaron Ogden, I'll pass on your concerns. Now, here is the form for you to complete. Since the copier is obviously not working, you'll need to complete the form three times so we have what we need for our records. Each form will need to be identical."

After we complete the form in triplicate, we return to the desk. Mrs. Daniels looks over each form as if she's grading a dissertation. She has us make several corrections in places she deems "not exact." Mostly, I think she's being a snot head.

Finally, she says, "You can leave now. Whoever responds to this will go to you if there are any questions."

"That's fine, Mrs. Daniels," Aaron says. "My apartment address is on there, but I'm spending quite a bit of time at my parents' house. Laurie and I are..." His voice fades off slightly, then he says, "Laurie is staying there for the summer."

"Oh, I'm sure you're spending plenty of time there, with your parents out of town and all. What is it they say? When the cat's away the mouse will play? Oh, believe me, I know all about you and those like you, Aaron Ogden. At least Laurie's been around the block a time or two and isn't a poor innocent young girl for you to take advantage of, like Tabby was."

My jaw drops. *I've been around the block a time or two?* Every noise in the building seems to stop, and I can feel all eyes on us. Poor Aaron. He's still holding his head high, but there's a slight twitch along his eye. I take his hand and quietly say, "Let's go."

Apparently, the wrath of Mrs. Daniels isn't finished. "You should be ashamed of yourself, Ogden. The way you ruined Tabitha's reputation and then destroyed her parents, why I never—"

"That's enough," I bark. "You're such a...such a busybody. But you really don't even know what you're talking about. You're nothing but a...nothing but a snot head. Let's go, Aaron."

As we hustle to the door, with me practically dragging Aaron in my rush to get away, Mrs. Daniels yells, "How dare you talk to me that way! Your mom would be ashamed of you, Laurie Esplin. Ashamed. Talking to a friend of hers in such a manner."

I turn around, straightening to my full five foot, five inches, and say as calmly as I can muster, "You, Monica Daniels, are no friend to my mom. You're nothing but a backstabbing, conniving gossip. Your opinion of me isn't needed or wanted. Now, how about you just do your job for a change? The entire town of Wesley has heard about how you keep your employment. We all know it isn't because you have any skills or real work ethic. Oh, unless gossiping is a skill. If that was the case—"

"Enough, Laurie," Aaron says. "Let's go." He takes my hand and begins to walk away from the door, gently towing me behind.

"Not yet." I raise my voice to ensure she hears me. "I wasn't finished telling her how we all know about her and the former police chief!"

"Laurie!" Aaron firmly whispers. "Enough. Stop. You're better than that. Better than her."

Chapter 19

I bite my lip as the tears start flowing. I'm mad. When I get mad, I can't help but cry. I hate it. At least the tears stayed away long enough that I could give her a small piece of my mind. I'm glad Aaron stopped me; I really don't want to lower myself to her level. Well, right now I want to, but I'd feel badly about it later.

Aaron opens the car door for me, holding it while I get in. I rummage in his glove box, looking for a napkin to wipe my eyes and blow my nose, while he comes around. He sits in the driver's seat, buckling the seatbelt, but makes no motion to start the truck.

I manage to pull myself together enough to say, "I'm sorry. I know I should've just walked away. But she's such a mean person. She's never happy unless she's bringing someone else down."

"There's some truth to the things she said about me," Aaron says quietly.

"What? That Tabby was innocent and you corrupted her? Ha. Keep in mind she used to date my old boyfriend Grant's younger brother. Believe me, I know she was far from innocent."

"That doesn't matter." Aaron gives a slight wave of his hand. "I was definitely a willing participant in everything Tabitha and I, uh…did."

We sit quietly for several minutes before Aaron says, "I've never really given you the details of what happened. I know you know the basics, but we've never really…" He lets out a big sigh. "I've never shared exactly what happened."

He's right. He hasn't told me. I've heard all of the rumors—pretty much everyone in town has, thanks to Monica Daniels and others like her—and I know what Aaron's parents and other people I trust know. Aaron has told me quite a bit, but not everything. I look at him expectantly.

He nods. "I've been wanting to tell you, but the timing never seemed quite right. You and I…you know I loved you long before I met Tabitha."

I nod and start to answer, but he lifts his hand and continues, "And when you and I started seeing each other after…afterwards. It was just not something I wanted to talk about. I mean, really, we've known each other forever, so how could I talk about something like this? I wanted to think you already knew and that was enough. But it's not. Not enough."

"Aaron, I'm okay with you telling me anything you want. But I'm also okay with you not sharing everything. You and Tabby were married. Husbands and wives often have their own secrets, things not to be shared with others. There isn't any reason for me to know those things."

"But that's just it, Laurie. Our marriage wasn't…it wasn't like that. It's no secret she didn't want to marry me. When she told me she was pregnant, she followed it up with 'I'm getting an abortion. You need to drive me to Billings.' I was shocked."

My eyes go wide. I didn't know about her wanting an abortion. Aaron nods in response to my reaction. "Yeah. I told her I couldn't do that and if she didn't want the baby, I'd raise it. She didn't have to have anything to do with him or her. And she didn't have to have anything to do with me. Just have the baby and I'd take care of everything else. She told me she'd think about it, but I couldn't call her or anything until she let me know her decision. It was two days before she called. Those were a terrible two days. I didn't know if she had a friend take her to the abortion clinic or what was happening. I didn't know—" Aaron gulps. "I didn't know if my child was still living."

"But she didn't have the abortion."

"She didn't have the abortion." He nods with a small, sad smile. "She agreed to carry the baby to term and let me raise him. We waited several weeks before we told our parents. We told my mom and dad first. They readily agreed to help with anything we'd need, and would help me raise the baby. Then we told her parents. That didn't go as well. As you know, her dad insisted we get married. Her mom would've preferred to ship Tabitha away and have the baby put up for adoption. She said it'd be easier than having to see the baby with me or my family in town."

While I didn't know Tabitha threatened abortion, the rest of this story isn't a surprise. I've heard all of it through the family grapevine. "So…you got married."

He nods. "On paper. We weren't...it wasn't a real marriage. We didn't..." he shakes his head, "not since we found out she was pregnant. We weren't intimate after that, not even on our wedding night or honeymoon. I know I probably shouldn't tell you these things, but you should know."

I have terribly mixed emotions. Part of me is happy he wasn't with her again, but mostly I'm sad he had a marriage without physical intimacy. The closeness and physical contact lacking in our relationship is tough, but to be married and not have it...I shake my head.

"When we got back from our honeymoon, we moved into her parents' guest cottage. I slept on the couch. I still tried to be a good husband, do things for her like my dad does for my mom. You know what a great relationship they have."

"They do. Your parents are great together. My parents too. We've been fortunate to have a healthy marriage modeled for us."

"Yeah. But Tabitha was just so unhappy. We'd been home less than a month when she had a doctor's appointment. I took the day off to go with her. She didn't care one way or another. She was less than enthused when we showed up for our 10:00 am appointment. After the nurse did her stuff, Dr. Mathews came in. She did a few things, then listened for the heartbeat. I don't know what she heard, but after a few minutes, she said, 'Let's do an ultrasound today. We haven't done one since you were ten weeks.' Tabitha just shrugged, but I was excited I'd get to see our baby."

I unbuckle my seatbelt and twist in my seat, pulling my leg up and trying to get comfortable. This isn't a part of the family grapevine I've heard, and I have to wonder why he's telling me about this.

"After a few minutes, the doctor and her nurse came back in. They got Tabitha situated and started the ultrasound. I tried getting a look at the monitor, but they had it turned so I couldn't see it. Tabitha stared at the ceiling and didn't even pretend to be interested. Finally, after what felt like forever, Dr. Mathews said, 'We need to have a more extensive ultrasound performed. I need you to go to the hospital in Prospect.' Tabitha groaned and said, 'Fine. When?' and Dr. Mathews asked us to leave her office and go straight to the hospital.

"I started to freak out, wondering what exactly they saw on the ultrasound. I tried asking, but Dr. Mathews insisted she'd meet us there and we'd find out more as soon as possible. I barely remember the drive. Tabitha was hungry and had me go through the McDonalds first. Then, when we got there, they admitted her—put her in a room and everything. I had a very bad feeling then. A nurse came in and did a question and answer session. Again, Tabitha didn't seem too concerned. She was detached and monotone in her answers."

Aaron pauses and grabs his water bottle out of the cup holder. After a long drink, he says, "Finally, Dr. Mathews showed up with the tech and a much larger ultrasound machine. She said something like, 'We'll get some answers, then we can make a decision how next to proceed.' I couldn't help but ask if our baby was going to die. Out of the corner of my eye, I thought I saw a slight lift to Tabitha's mouth, a small smile. But I don't know for sure."

Sucking in a breath, I look at Aaron. He didn't really say she was smiling at the prospect of their child dying, did he? She wouldn't. *Would she?*

"Dr. Mathews put me off and said, 'Let's finish the tests, then we'll talk.' I watched as they put some goop on Tabitha's stomach. No sooner did the ultrasound wand touch the goop, her stomach quivered. Dr. Mathews and the ultrasound tech both said 'Whoa, did you see that?' Then they looked at the screen and broke into huge smiles.

"Tabitha sighed and, in a completely monotone voice, said, 'I guess everything is fine. The thing is kicking me.' Dr. Mathews confirmed everything looked fine and thought maybe something was wrong with the ultrasound machine in the office. Then she asked if we wanted to know the sex of our baby. Tabitha shrugged, so I said, 'Do you want to know? We can wait. I'm fine either way.' She said it didn't matter. And...you know he's a boy."

I feel a tear running down my cheek as I smile. "I know he's a boy."

Aaron's eyes are filled with tears as he gives a slow nod. "So they discharged us. We drove home. I tried to talk with her, but she'd only grunt her responses. When we got back to the house, she went straight to the bedroom. After a while, I knocked on the door and told her I was going to make something to eat. She mumbled back something, which sounded like *whatever*. When the food was ready, she came out and ate without talking to me at all, even when I'd talk to her directly. Then she went back in the bedroom and—"

"Hey, Aaron! What are you doing here?" Master Shane's booming voice causes both of us to jump.

Chapter 20

Aaron quickly wipes his eyes and pastes on a smile. "Oh, yes, hello. I was filing a report."

"What for?" he asks.

"Someone shot at him!" I answer.

"What? When?" Master Shane looks around, crouching slightly.

"Earlier," Aaron says, then goes on to tell the story of the campers.

"So you put in your paperwork with Secretary Ratched?"

"Secretary Ratched?" I ask.

"You know, that..." Master Shane appears to be searching for the proper word. He rarely uses colorful language, feeling it shows a lack of discipline, but I've heard the rare expletive from him. The way he looks now makes me think he might be coming up with a profanity. Instead, he says, "Forgive me. I know Monica Daniels from the city police is covering the front desk. She can be rather...intense."

I snort and mutter, "You ain't kidding."

Aaron lightly touches my arm, then asks, "What are you doing here, sir?"

"Heard about the trouble they're having in Prospect. Hustled down to see if I could help. But *Mrs. Daniels* made it completely clear that an old retired guy like me would be of no use. I am to leave it to the professionals. I'm a civilian now, and I'd better start acting like one."

"How'd you hear about Prospect?" Aaron asks, as I say, "What kind of trouble are they having?"

"I pulled out my old analog police scanner, just to see if it worked. Managed to pick up enough info to know something big is happening in Prospect. But what exactly is going on, I'm not sure. And since I'm a civilian now, *she*—" he jerks his thumb back toward the building "—won't tell me. I guess that's fair. Except," he huffs out a breath. "Except, what I did hear tells me my old coworkers, *my friends*, might be in trouble."

"We might need to go to Prospect later today," I say. "A boy from my neighborhood was beat up the other night. He's in the hospital."

"Toby something? I heard about that. Stopped by the other day to check on you, but you weren't around."

77

"How'd you hear?" I ask, instantly realizing he may be a civilian now, but he still has connections.

"Dan Mansen—ran into him yesterday morning. Toby's not the only one. There have been several incidents. People living at the river, though...I hadn't heard about that. I'm heading over to Dan's house. Pretty sure he's in Prospect, but if he's not, he'll want to take care of the river situation quickly. The guy might not miss next time."

"Thank you, Master," I say. "That's our concern too."

"Yep. Say, were you two using my range on Sunday?"

"We were, sir," Aaron answers. "I thought it'd be okay, even if you weren't there."

"Absolutely. Probably smart to get in some practice time. In fact, why don't you two come over tomorrow? I'd like to teach you a few other things."

"Like what?" I ask.

"Defensive shooting."

"Um, isn't that what we did? The whole reason Aaron took me there was so I could become more comfortable with the pistol and shotgun, in case I need to shoot for self-defense."

Master nods. "That's true. But I bet what you did was carefully line up on the target, make sure your sights were in place, maybe take a breath or two—three even, then finally fire your weapon. Right?"

I shrug, as Aaron nods and says, "Yes, sir. That's pretty much how we practiced."

"Right. That's pretty much how everyone approaches target shooting. But if you're being attacked, will you have time to go through your process? Nope. You'll only have a second or two to draw your weapon and fire. That's defensive shooting. I'll help you with it. In fact," he looks at the sky for a moment, "let's do it today. Say, an hour and a half? That work?"

Aaron looks at me; I give a slight nod. "Sounds fine, sir," he says. "Mind if we bring some containers to collect water?"

"Nope, not at all. Heard the city water is just about done for. Not sure what's going to happen after that. Maybe Dan will know what the plan is."

"See you soon," I say, trying to add more enthusiasm to my voice than I'm feeling. I'm getting a lump in my stomach at the thought of needing to use defensive shooting—especially in our little town of Wesley.

Our little town where my fiancé was shot at this morning.

Chapter 21

We go back to the house for breakfast and, finally, coffee. It was amazing. I didn't even mind the coffee grounds getting stuck in my teeth.

My dad would always toss the last bit of coffee left in his cup. One time, I asked him why he does it that way. He said, when he was younger, he didn't have a fancy coffee maker. His coffee maker boiled the coffee, and he'd often have coffee grounds in his cup. They sank to the bottom, so he'd dump out the last swallow to avoid getting a mouthful of grounds. I now see the wisdom in that.

After breakfast, and flossing to remove the coffee bits, we work on finishing the master bathroom organization. Again, we divide things up, part for his apartment and part staying here.

"You have enough space at your place for all the things we're taking over?" I ask.

"I'm okay, for now. At least the medicine cabinet stuff is small. We should be able to do at least one of the other three bathrooms before we go to Master Shane's place for shooting class."

"About that—you really think it's necessary? The way he said he should teach us to shoot?"

"It makes sense. You know my shooting experience is limited to hunting. I've never really thought about needing to shoot to defend my life—to defend *your* life. But after this morning, yeah, it's necessary."

I feel my shoulders sag and the lump in my stomach returning. Even if I have this training, would I actually use it? Could I pull a gun on someone?

I've been taking martial arts for over a dozen years. It wasn't until I was several years into my training that I realized it could be used for self-defense. I was a sophomore in high school watching an MMA fight on pay-per-view with some classmates. It was amazing to see so many of the kicking moves I knew—not just knew but was really good at—being used by these fighters. I went to my next practice elated over this epiphany, excited to tell Master Shane what I'd discovered.

He was very kind as he pointed out what he already knew; Taekwondo can definitely be used as a form of self-defense.

It was shortly after this that our trainings changed, with him often mentioning how Taekwondo could be used for defense. Around that time, Master Shane started studying Yongmudo—a discipline primarily focused on self-defense—through several in-depth training courses.

Currently, he's a seventh dan black belt in Taekwondo and a fourth dan in Yongmudo. When he first started teaching Yongmudo, after he received his first black belt, he encouraged me to join. But I was so busy with work and doing Taekwondo two nights per week—plus the occasional weekend tournament—I didn't want to take on anything more.

Now, I wonder. If I would've learned a martial art more focused on defense, would I feel better about this? I don't think so. I think the bottom line is, I don't want to ever have to take the life of another person. Nope. I couldn't do it—not under any circumstance.

Aaron and I take care of the half bath off the laundry room and the full basement bathroom before heading out to Master Shane's place. There's not much in either room, so they go quick. We load up every empty water container we find and take them to the bed of Aaron's truck. When we're almost ready, he says, "I was thinking it might be smart if we left a few things at Bill's house."

"What kind of things?"

"Stuff like what we're dividing between us—medical supplies, clothes, maybe even guns."

"You're sounding a little…" I search my mind for the right word.

"Paranoid?" Aaron offers.

I give a combination of a nod and a shrug.

"Yep. I think you're right. I am, but let's do it anyway. Maybe even drop a few things at the dojang."

I shake my head, thinking it sounds ridiculous, but say, "Whatever you think."

When we pull up to Master Shane's house, once again greeted by Freckles, I'm shocked at the changes he's made. Like the martial arts studio, he's covered all the windows with plywood. The beautiful—and usually inviting—porch across the front has a layer of sandbags up against the railing. It looks like a war zone instead of someplace to relax and enjoy a visit.

"C'mon in, you two," he says, hanging halfway out the door. "Let's fill up your water containers before we get to it."

Inside the house, there are more sandbags stacked up under the windows. The windows are all open and the screens have been removed. Looking closer, I notice there are holes in the plywood. *What is Master Shane expecting to happen here?* In one corner of the dining room are several rolls of barbed wire fencing, plastic containers of screws, and boxes of nails.

"Putting up a fence?" I ask.

"Something like that," Master Shane says with a nod.

"The plywood, it won't..." Aaron pauses, then quickly asks, "It won't stop a bullet, will it?"

"Nope, probably not. Well, maybe a .22 caliber or something similarly light from a distance. The sandbags are for cover. They'll stop bullets. The plywood is so people can't see what's going on in here."

"And the holes?" I ask, feeling I already know the answer.

"Shooting ports." Master Shane shrugs. "I still need to cover the sections of the plywood with holes with black trash bags."

"What for?" I ask.

"Thought they could act as blackout curtains. That way, if I have a lamp on in here, it won't be noticed. I didn't think of that until last night when I was outside with Freckles and looked back. The little holes glittered like stars because of the lanterns lighting up my living room."

"And then you can just rip down the trash bag if you need to use the shooting ports?" I gulp at the thought of it.

Master shrugs, giving a small nod. I guess he doesn't really like the thought of it either.

I look around the house to see if there are other changes. His place is beautiful. A real log cabin built from dead standing pine he ordered from a small lumber mill. He acted as general contractor and main laborer during the process. According to him, the house is still not completely finished, but it looks amazing to me.

The front door opens into the combination living room, dining room, and kitchen. The open floor plan makes the small space seem quite large. There's a beautiful rock fireplace with a woodstove insert on the wall opposite the kitchen. At the back of the house is a lovely staircase going up to the loft area, which is set up as an office and guest room. There's a half bath upstairs also. Two bedrooms and a full bath are on the main level, tucked behind the staircase.

"So," Master Shane says, "before we go out to the range, let's talk about being prepared. Aaron, you always carry a pocketknife, right?"

"Sure." He shrugs. "I've carried one for years. It comes in handy."

"Let's see it."

Aaron pulls out his small pocketknife and shows it to Master. "Good. A nice little Buck knife. And I know you have a good edge on it, right?"

Aaron nods.

"What about you, Laurie? Do you have a pocketknife?"

I shake my head. "I've never had one."

Master bends down and lifts his pant leg slightly, exposing the top of his boot. "See that?" He points to the knife looped on the tongue part of his boot.

"That's nice," Aaron says while I nod.

"So do you have any boots like this?" Master asks me.

"No. I only have tennis shoes, sandals, and dress shoes. I have boots in my storage in Laramie…not exactly like that, but similar."

"Too bad. I have a few boot knives that would work for you. Aaron, I can give you one since you wear your work boots pretty much every day. We can get Laurie a pocketknife, which would be better than nothing."

"Why do I need a pocketknife?" I ask.

"Never know. It's always good to have options."

"I have several pocketknives," Aaron says. "I can help her pick one out."

"All right, that'll be fine. We'll focus on the pistol and shotgun today, but let's plan a time for you to come back and we'll talk about defensive knife practice."

I shake my head. These two—they act like Wesley is going to become a war zone or something.

After we fill up our water, he takes us to the shooting range. Master Shane has set things up a little differently, with several targets set up in a semicircle. The practice starts similar to the things Aaron and I did the other day, with lots of dry fire sessions so I can learn how to pull my weapon from my holster.

When we finally move on to live firing, I'm feeling much more comfortable. And I'm able to smoothly pull and discharge my weapon.

Overall, I'm pretty happy with how the day goes. And as long as I still continue to only think of it as firing at a target, I'm good.

Chapter 22

By the time we finish the shooting drills, we're late for our 2:00 visit at the clinic to find out about picking up Toby. Well, *I* think we're late. Aaron reminds me they said to check *after* 2:00 for an update.

Both the clinic parking lot and waiting room are full. The line to the desk starts right outside the front door. It's mostly orderly, but many people are injured with limbs that look broken, cuts, lots of coughing, and a few people have blisters.

Is there a new poison of some sort going around causing the coughing and blisters? They messed with our water and food; is there now some sort of bioattack?

I share my concerns with Aaron; he leans in and whispers, "I don't think so. I think the blisters are from burns and the coughing is from smoke damage."

"A fire? Where?"

Aaron shrugs. It's several minutes before the line moves enough for us to enter the building. The chairs are full and people are sitting on the floor. Almost everyone's either crying or making moaning noises.

"So many people," I say. "What's happening?"

"Mayhem," Aaron whispers.

Jane, the nurse from the other night, is one of three people at the desk. She catches my eye and gives a deep frown. *What's that about?*

Waiting in the disorganized line, we start picking up bits and pieces of the conversations going on around us. Seems whatever happened in Prospect has brought people here for treatment. That makes absolutely zero sense to me, since Prospect has an actual hospital. Like with the case of Toby, seriously injured people are shipped to Prospect; Prospect doesn't ship their injured to this small clinic. We watch as clinic personnel call people back to the small treatment area.

More and more people file in. A young girl, who appears seriously injured, is rushed back. Another time, someone comes in screaming for help—probably the same way Cheyenne did when we brought Toby here—and one of the nurses behind the desk drops everything to help. Aaron was right—mayhem.

After what seems like forever, we finally reach the desk. One of the others, not Jane, asks if she can help us. Jane touches her arm and says, "Let's switch, I'll help them."

Without preamble, Aaron asks, "What's going on?"

"There's a problem in Prospect, a problem at the hospital."

"What kind of problem?" I ask.

"We don't really have the exact details, but it seems a gunfight or something broke out. Then, somehow, the hospital caught on fire."

"Oh no."

Jane nods. "We don't know much yet. Prospect is having the same trouble as we are with their water system, so putting out the fire isn't—" She pauses for a moment, closing her eyes. When she opens them, her voice cracks as she says, "They aren't doing very well with putting out the fire."

"Do we know—"

"We don't know anything. We haven't been able to get much information. People started showing up here to get treatment for their burns. We aren't set up for this, but we're doing our best. We lost contact with the hospital hours ago, so we didn't even…" She shakes her head. "I don't know about your friend. We hope to find out when things calm down."

"When do you think we should come back?" Aaron asks.

She shrugs, then looks thoughtful for a moment. "Hey, Laurie. Don't you work for Dr. Anderson?"

I nod and she says, "He's here. Dr. Ford had Thad go find him, to have him help. Thad got the other two dentists and all of the town's veterinarians also."

"How do you have room for everyone?" Aaron asks.

She leans in and whispers, "We're using the firehouse next door too. They moved the ambulance and all the fire trucks out. We've set things up as best we can. It's still not great. Laurie, maybe you can help? You've worked with Dr. Anderson. You can assist him."

What? No. "Umm, I don't…you see, mainly, I answer phones. I help in the back office if someone's off, but I'm not an *actual* assistant."

She tilts her head to the side. "Wait. You're premed, right? You're going to UW, then going to medical school. I remember now."

"No, I'm predentistry. Big difference."

Aaron leans over and whispers, "You could help. It'd be good to help."

86

I shake my head, but my mouth says, "Fine. Where's Dr. Anderson. I'll go ask *him* if he thinks I can be of any help."

"Good. Go back out the front, then over to the firehouse. Go in the side door. The bays will be shut. Better to go that way than try to get through the way we're taking people. It's a madhouse back there."

"Aaron's going with me."

"Sure, of course." Her eyes leave mine, and to the next person in line, she says, "What can I do for you today?"

Aaron and I make our way out the door. The line of people is now stretching well into the parking lot. There's also now a nurse—at least, I assume she's a nurse—set up at a table by the front door. She sends the less injured into the line. Those who are more injured avoid the line and wait for a gurney or stretcher to arrive to transport them. We find Dr. Anderson exactly where Jane said we would. He asks me to stay and help. Aaron's also put to work.

My job is to follow Dr. Anderson around, essentially acting as his gopher. Not an easy task when I don't know where anything is. Aaron becomes an orderly, helping Thad and the others move people around. There are two others who work for Dr. Anderson that are also helping: the main dental assistant and one of our hygienists. There are also several other town people who are offering their assistance that work at vet's offices, other dental offices, pharmacies, and even nursing homes. Whoever rounded up help did a very good job of finding people with any sort of medical experience.

I quickly discover the injured we're seeing are only a drop in the bucket of the number of people injured in Prospect. Those critically injured are being taken straight to Cody or Billings, Montana. Those seriously injured but not considered critical are mostly being taken to Pryor, about thirty miles up the road, heading toward the mountains. They have a small twenty-bed acute care hospital with an emergency room. We're seeing people who are injured, but not severely—for the most part.

While we don't have contact with Prospect, the radio system can still reach the town of Pryor and is in contact with good ole Monica Daniels at the sheriff substation. To her credit, she does relay essential information as she gets it.

Even though we're not supposed to have those seriously injured, a few people on their way to Pryor were apparently in worse condition than the triage in Prospect thought. They ran into trouble before getting there and stopped for emergency treatment. The little girl who was brought back when we were originally waiting in line to find out about Toby is one of those. She's declared dead at 8:17 PM.

I wasn't caring for her, but it's still heartbreaking. Sadly, she's one of four that dies. Finally, at midnight, we're told we can leave.

"Is there any way I can find out about my neighbor?" I ask Dr. Anderson.

"Not tonight, Laurie. We don't know when we'll know about the patients and staff at the hospital. Rumor is…" He gulps in a breath. "You've heard the rumors, right?"

"Hundreds dead," I whisper.

He nods. "We don't think they were able to get many patients out, not ones who were admitted and on the higher floors, anyway. I'm sorry, Laurie, but the people we're seeing are ones who were in the walk-in clinic or emergency room and a couple of people from the soup kitchen the hospital Chaplain was operating out of the cafeteria."

"Yeah, I talked with one of the women who was helping serve food. She said the Chaplain was amazing, the way he locked down the cafeteria as soon as they heard the shooting. Then he kept everyone calm and organized when the fire started, taking them out a side door. She was only injured because she went back to try to retrieve the food. Did you see the Chaplain? Is he here?"

"No, seems after he got the cafeteria people out, he went into the main building to help move people. Thad said he heard he saved dozens, but it's feared he didn't make it out the final time."

I feel myself choking up, again. I've been brought to tears so many times since I started helping today, but I've managed to keep myself together. Even when the little girl died, I didn't cry.

"Maybe he's fine and still helping people in Prospect," I say. "Why'd they have a soup kitchen going anyway? Are people already out of food?"

"I understand it was mainly for the vacationers. Just like every summer, the population swelled with people visiting Yellowstone and the Big Horns. You know how it is."

I do know how it is. Like Cody to the south of us, Prospect gets an influx of summer travelers. Our county relies on tourism as a main industry. Even so, the locals complain about it every year. I'm no different. I hate having to go into Prospect during the summer months.

"That makes sense," I agree. "Maybe Toby is one of the ones who got out. We don't know what floor he was on. And he was probably well enough he could walk out on his own, right?"

Dr. Anderson puts a hand on my shoulder and gives me a sad smile. "Maybe so, Laurie. Go on home, get some sleep. They're letting me go too. Just keeping the real doctors and nurses around for tonight. Seems they figure they can function better with little sleep than us lazy dentists and veterinarians." He gives a weak smile at his lame joke.

I start to walk toward Aaron, standing by the door, but after a couple of steps, I stop and turn back to Dr. Anderson. "Do you think I'll get to finish school? Become a dentist? Or is this," I gesture to the building, our new world, "is this it? We're going to have disaster after disaster here until...until what?"

"I don't know, Laurie. I truly don't know. If there's any good news from today, it's that we didn't hear reports of any new terrorist attacks."

I nod. "Well, I guess that's something then. Goodnight, Dr. Anderson."

Aaron drives me home. Finally giving in to my emotions, I cry as soon as I get in his truck. He walks me into the house and turns on my battery-operated lantern, then lights several of the candles I have around the living room.

Aaron's mom had a candle making business a few years ago; she made beeswax and other types of candles to sell at farmers markets and craft shows. I pull out some of these jar candles from her storage cabinet to use for lighting. Aaron took several to his place also, and we divided up the pillar, votive, and taper candles to use when the jar candles are depleted.

"I wish I could take a hot bath." I collapse onto the couch.

"You going to be okay?"

Will I be okay?

"Yeah. Sleep will help. Do me a favor and don't come over until 10:00 or so tomorrow, okay? I want to sleep in."

"Sure. Might even be a little bit later," he says. "Thad asked if I could help clean up in the morning. They figure the people they have sleeping in the firehouse tonight will be able to leave in the morning. They tried to put the most severely injured in the clinic rooms. I'm going to help put the firehouse back together."

"Why bother? It's not like the fire trucks and ambulance can go anywhere—not without water to put out a fire or fuel to run the vehicles."

Aaron shrugs. "I told him I'd help."

After he leaves, I grab a package of wet wipes and clean up as best I can. I smell like smoke, and other things I don't care to identify. The chemical scent of the wet wipes is only a minor improvement. I change into shorts and a T-shirt before crawling into bed shortly after 1:30. I'm sleeping as late as I want in the morning. My body—and mind—needs the rest.

The screaming and pounding on the door wake me up.

Chapter 23

I'm at the bottom of the stairs with my hand on the doorknob, before I'm awake enough to realize I should've grabbed the handgun. The shotgun is in the hall closet behind me. The banging on the door hasn't stopped, neither have the shouts for help. I peek out the side window. There's just enough moonlight to make out the person on the porch.

Heather. I open the door and she falls into me. I drag her inside, using my foot to shut the door.

"Thank you! Oh, thank you! They're crazy. We have to go...somewhere. They want to hurt me. Oh—"

"Heather, stop. I don't know what's going on. Who wants to hurt you?"

"It's them! They—"

The door crashes open. We're slammed against the wall, pinned behind the door.

"Heather, you've been a very bad girl," Jeremy, the thug who beat up Toby, says in a sing-song voice. "You've got some 'splainin' to do."

"No!" Heather cries, burying her face in my shoulder. "Leave me alone!"

In the dark, he makes a rough grab for her, trying to pull her away. I hold on to her as he yanks.

"Stop it!" I yell. "Leave her alone!"

I don't see him ball up his fist, but the punch hits me hard directly below my right cheek. My head snaps to the side, hitting the spindle. I loosen my grip on Heather. He yanks her away. I've been hit before when sparring without my gear, but it was always an accident—and rarely this hard.

As I try to get to my feet, hands grab at me, yanking me up. Chuck—the guy who made my drinks at the bonfire and participated in Toby's beating. Are the others here too? There were three others with them that night.

"Hey there, Laurie," Chuck says in a totally calm and cool voice. These guys must have some mental issues, based on the way they

91

respond to the violence they're inflicting. I rip my arm out of his grasp and quickly get my balance.

My eyes are adjusting to the darkness. I can just make out Jeremy with Heather pulled tight against him, his hand covering her mouth as he whispers in her ear. Her eyes are wide and wild; she frantically shakes her head.

Chuck laughs at me. "Whoa there, gurl. You're quite the little rascal, aren't you?" Jeremy joins in the laughing. I can feel tears stinging my eyelids. I blink a few times, then straighten my shoulders. He doesn't grab for me again, but Chuck is very close—invading my space, his hot breath laden with booze and the sweet, sickly smell of marijuana.

"Let her go," I say quietly.

Jeremy and Chuck laugh harder. "Oh, sure," Jeremy says, "I'll let her go—in just a bit. But first—" His laugh stops, and his eyes turn completely cold. "First, it looks like we need to have an attitude adjustment for both of you."

Heather stomps on his foot. He bends over slightly. She throws her head back, hitting him in the lip. I take advantage of her attack to elbow strike Chuck in the sternum, then use my left hand for a palm strike to his chin. I back up against the wall to put a little distance between myself and Chuck, raising my leg in a push kick to his gut. This sends him flying off the elevated entry area, into the living room. He lands with a thump on his backside, hitting his shoulder on the back of the couch. I don't expect the laugh he emits.

Out of the corner of my eye, I see Jeremy grab Heather by the hair; she cries out. He's just within range for a side kick with my left leg to his hip. He yelps, throws Heather against the wall, and then turns to me. "You're a feisty one, aren't you?"

Chuck is back on his feet, and says, "Dang, gurl. You sure know your foreplay." They both laugh in their crazy, insane way. Heather is crumpled on the floor, wailing. I'm well balanced in fighting stance, but so cramped in the entry way that I can't make any sort of move.

And there's two of them. I've gone against two attackers as part of my training, but it was training. We have rules when we train. I'm under no illusions these two have any sort of rules.

Jeremy snarls and says, "Well, then. I'm always a fan of leading up to things slowly, but enough is enough. Chuck, grab the wench."

92

Chuck laughs slightly, rubbing his shoulder. "Let me find some rope. I'm tying those feet up."

Jeremy grabs Heather again. "Oh, I think she'll be a little calmer now, won't you, Laurie?" He licks Heather, his tongue moving slowly from her jaw to her temple. Heather whimpers and tries to pull away, which results in him pulling her closer. "Now, now, Heather." He gives me a hard look. "Do we have an understanding?"

Oh, I understand all right. I understand Heather and I are in trouble. Why didn't I lock the door as soon as I had her inside? Why didn't I bring the handgun down with me? Can I get to the shotgun? It's in the coat closet, a door in the living room right next to the basement door.

I raise my hands in surrender. "I understand."

He gives me a creepy smile. "Where can Chuck find some rope?"

"I don't know. I-I can't think of any. Maybe in the garage or the shed in the back?"

Chuck laughs. "I don't think so. Bet we can find something in the kitchen. Maybe we should move them both to the couch. It's easier to watch them if they're close together."

"Or maybe we should just get on with it," Jeremy says, his tongue tracing the same path as before.

Chapter 24

Jeremy follows Chuck's suggestion of moving us to the couch. Heather is nothing more than a lump; all the fight seems to have left her. As they're moving us, I realize neither Jeremy nor Chuck have shown us a weapon. I haven't seen a gun, knife, or anything else on either of them. Jeremy has used his fists on us, but nothing else. Pretty weird they don't have something. Guns are very common in Wyoming. So common, in fact, it's not unusual to see people in the grocery store, dentist office, or even church with a sidearm.

Thank you, God. Thank you for them not being armed.

Chuck moves around the living room, lighting candles and turning on my single battery-operated lantern.

Jeremy sits on the fireplace hearth, leering at us. "That's enough light," he says. "Take one of those candles with you while you find the rope. You're probably right about there being something in the kitchen. Duct tape would work too."

"Yep. I'll find something," Chuck says, leaving the room. He starts his drawer rummaging, which includes a running commentary as he mutters to himself. Aaron and I have already gone through those drawers, removing everything we thought we could use and storing it all together on a shelf in the basement or at Aaron's apartment. There was a small roll of kitchen string, duct tape, and mailing tape.

"This is the most organized kitchen I've ever seen," he yells. "She might be right. I'll need to go to the garage."

"Skip it," Jeremy says. "I'm sure she's going to be a good girl, aren't you, Laurie?"

I give him a look that I hope relays my exact thoughts. It must because he laughs and says, "She's a feisty one all right. Maybe she does need to be tied up."

I drop my eyes and scoot close to Heather, tossing a throw blanket stretched out across the back of the couch so it's out of the way. "No need," I say. The last thing I want is to be tied up. I scan the area, looking for anything we can use as a weapon. Argh! Why didn't I bring the pistol with me? *Stupid, stupid, stupid.*

"You say that now, but I'm quickly learning you can't be trusted. Go ahead, Chuck. See what you can find."

I realize this might be the opportunity we need to get away—Jeremy, alone without any weapons. I can take him. *I'm sure I can.* Then I'll grab Heather, and we'll escape out the front door. It's a good plan. But can we make it work? A quick look at Heather and I wonder if she even has the ability to run out the door.

"I'll be right back," Chuck says. "You can handle them both?"

Jeremy eyeballs me. "I'm sure I can. Heather, why don't you move over here by me? That should give Laurie a little inspiration to mind her manners."

Not fair!

Heather reluctantly stands and sits next to Jeremy. He puts his arm around her and pulls her tight. "Go ahead, Chuck."

He opens a door, then slams it shut. "That was the pantry. Where's the garage?"

"The other door. Go through the laundry room," I say through gritted teeth.

The door opens with a loud squeak. "Found it," Chuck says.

As soon as the door shuts, Heather lifts her head. She gives me a look I interpret as *let's do this* and immediately throws herself on the carpeted floor.

"Hey, you!" Jeremy roars, bending over and reaching for a lank of hair. She flips onto her back and kicks him in the thigh, landing a glancing blow, then scrambles away. At the same time, I'm off the sofa and in position for a roundhouse. Just like when sparring with the practice bag, I move in close for the kick with my right leg, aiming low to catch him in the temple. His head snaps to the left. I follow it with an immediate kick from my left. His head slams back to the right.

"Get out of here," I yell at Heather. I lift my right knee high, then thrust my hips forward, delivering a forward push kick. *Bullseye.* Smack on the tip of his nose, immediately rearranging his facial composition. With my fist in my left palm, I deliver a blow to his chin with the bony part of my right elbow. The momentum snaps his head back. There's a sickening crack as the back of his head slams into the hearth.

What have I done? I choke back a cry. "Let's go." I bend down and grab Heather off the floor.

Her eyes are wide as she says, "Is he—did you—"

Strong hands grab me from behind. "What did you do?" Chuck yells.

He tosses me to the side, throwing me into the side table next to the sofa. I hit my eye hard as the table turns over.

"Jeremy! Jeremy, man!" Chuck lets out a roar. Heather starts screaming. He's on top of her, pummeling her, hitting her with his fists. He straddles her, picks up her head, and slams it into the floor. I struggle to my feet, then barrel into him. I catch him at enough of an angle to knock him off of her. I quickly right myself, moving into fighting stance. With a growl, he uses a side chair to help himself up.

I don't let him get to his feet before I deliver a spinning back kick to his temple, throwing him into the side table. The table breaks, knocking everything—including a lit candle—onto the floor. While he's down, I deliver a double side kick—two fast back-to-back kicks, making sure my heel catches him in the nose each time. Eyes closed, he slumps back.

At least there wasn't a sickening crack this time.

I grab for the throw blanket to tamp out the small fire the candle started. As I turn, I see flames behind me. The table I crushed had a candle on it too; the throw blanket is ablaze and the couch is on fire.

I move to Heather. Eyes closed, her head is nestled in a pool of blood. I glance over at Jeremy; there's a pool of blood around him also. Only his eyes are open, staring into nothingness. *I can't believe I-I killed him.*

I shake Heather; she doesn't move. Grabbing her shirt at the shoulders, I begin dragging her to the kitchen. Once we're on the smooth tile, moving is easier. I slide open the back door and get her out to the deck. As carefully as I can, I take her down the steps of the deck.

Once she is safely on the lawn and well away from the house, I start to go back inside for Chuck and Jeremy. After a few steps, I stop. What am I doing? Trying to save two guys who wanted to—to what? Other than the obvious, did they intend to kill us?

"Are you okay? Is there anyone still in the house?" I jump at the voice. I look around, frantically trying to find the speaker.

"Up here. It's me, Kim Hendrick, your neighbor." I look up to the second floor of the house next door. Kim gives me a wave. "Gene's going to the front. Is anyone still in the house?"

"Two guys," I answer. "They attacked us. I—" I gulp. "I think one is dead."

The shock on her face is evident. "Gene," she yells, "there are two guys in the house. They attacked them."

I can't hear her husband's response. I check Heather. She's still out. She's breathing but not very well. I'm torn with what to do; help Gene or stay with Heather? I start to stand, when Kim yells, "There's others from the neighborhood coming to help. I'll send someone to you. Wait there. Don't worry about the guys in the house. I just saw Gene come out with one of them. Bob Rodgers is going in now."

After only a minute or so, a neighbor from down the street is in the yard. He looks over Heather. "What happened?"

"He hit her and then banged her head into the floor. There's a lot of blood from her head. But head wounds bleed, right?"

He gently lifts her head, feeling the back with his fingers. The look on his face tells me something is wrong. "What?"

"We need to get her to the clinic. She's hurt pretty badly."

A second person shows up, and together they gently carry her to the front, lying her on the lawn.

"We can take my car," I say. "What about—what about the guys in the house?"

Kim's husband Gene says, "The one I brought out is alive, I think. The other one, he's dead."

Kim's no longer in the upstairs window. She's now standing on the lawn. My car keys are in the house, along with everything I own. I have a hidden key under the back fender. I start for it, when Kim says, "I'll take them in my truck. Gene, you'd better make sure the fire doesn't spread to our house, or Stoke's house on the other side. We can put the guy in the bed of the truck and the girl on the backseat." She peers at Heather. "Who is she?"

I stroke her blood-soaked hair and look over her battered face. "Heather...um, I can't remember her last name. She lives over there." I point to her house.

"Oh no," Kim says. "I didn't even...We'd better get going. Laurie, you need checked out too."

"What about my house?" I gesture to the still-burning structure.

"Not much we can do," Gene says. "Like Kim said, we'll make sure the fire doesn't spread. Rodger, can you ride in the bed of the truck? Keep the guy from causing any trouble?"

Rodger looks over Chuck and says, "Yeah, but I don't think he's going to be any trouble. What happened to him? Looks like his nose is shattered. He's got some smoke damage too. The broken nose isn't helping that."

Chapter 25

"Do you know what time it is?" I ask Kim from the backseat where I'm holding Heather. Her head is in my lap, the back of her head doesn't feel right. Instead of hard and bony, it's squishy. One of the neighbors wrapped her head in his T-shirt to help with the bleeding. Even so, I'm covered in blood. I lift my leg slightly to adjust how I'm holding her. When she noticed I was barefoot, Kim ran to her house and grabbed me a pair of flip-flops. They're more than one size too small and cutting into my feet.

"Just before 3:00," Kim answers.

A few minutes later, we pull into the parking lot. The clinic is considerably calmer than this afternoon, and even quieter than when Aaron and I left at midnight.

Will Aaron's parents' house burn to the ground? Or will it stop burning at some point? Either way, it's unlikely I can live there again.

A tired nursing staff helps us inside, where we're triaged in the waiting room. I insist I'm fine, and the nurse—one I worked with earlier—agrees. But I'm the only one who's fine.

Chuck's nose is shattered. He'll recover; the general consensus is he needs surgery to realign his nose. I guess a well-placed kick can do some serious damage. I shudder at the memory of the kick I gave Jeremy, which also shattered his nose. The sound of his head striking the hearth is something I'll never forget. Almost unconsciously, I massage my elbow. It's tender from the strike. I choose not to mention it.

Heather is unconscious and has a fractured skull. It's considered a severe fracture, with fluid leaking from both her nose and her ears. Shortly after we arrived, she had a seizure.

Both Heather and Chuck will be transported to Billings. This time, they didn't ask me for fuel. Maybe they have a donor or found a supply. Or maybe they realize I'm in no position to provide anything.

Dan Mansen, Master Shane's deputy friend, is talking with the doctor about Heather and Chuck. He tells me he'll be ready for my statement shortly. I nod morosely, sure I'm going to jail for killing

Jeremy. Even though it was self-defense, that's what they do, right? Put the suspect in jail and then sort it out later? I don't even try to stop my tears. My neighbor, Kim, tries to comfort me, but it does little good.

At the last minute, it was decided we should bring Jeremy's body, hauling it in the bed of the truck next to Chuck. Deputy Mansen checks him over, then takes my statement, which I manage to deliver between crying hiccups. Kim gives her statement.

Next, he interviews Chuck—his low baritone voice now a nasally mess, as he tries to play it off like Heather and I invited them to my house and freaked out on them. I guess Deputy Mansen doesn't believe him because Chuck is handcuffed for his ride to Billings.

"I stopped at your house first, got statements from the neighbors that were there. We'll get Heather's statement if...when she wakes up," Deputy Mansen tells me. "But for now, it's unlikely we'll move forward with any charges regarding the death."

"Thank you." I nod. "I feel terrible, but he was going to...they planned to...you know."

"Yes, I think I do know. When I got the radio call, I asked for the fire chief to be called also. He was at your place when I left. Gene Hendrick was instrumental in containing the fire. It didn't spread, but there isn't anything they can do for your house. Chief King thinks it will burn itself out within a few hours. If we get a rainstorm this afternoon, that'll really help."

I nod my understanding. I'm about to ask if he can give me a ride to Aaron's apartment when the front door of the clinic bursts open. It's Aaron, followed by Master Shane. Seconds later, I'm in Aaron's arms. He's saying all kinds of soothing words and telling me over and over how happy he is I'm okay and not to worry about anything else. All that matters is I'm safe.

"How'd you know?" I ask dumbly.

"Bill heard about it on his scanner."

"Yep," Master Shane says. "Woke up to Freckles barking at something—crazy dog. Decided to turn it on and see if I could get any more news about the incident in Prospect. Instead, I heard Chief King talking with Dan. They said it was the Ogden house and Dan had just left to go to the hospital and interview the occupants. Anyway, I picked up Aaron. Here we are."

I'm overcome with emotion; all I can do is cry and nod while Aaron holds me.

"Everything good, Dan?" Master Shane asks.

"Yep. I think I got what we need. The nurse wanted to talk to her again after I was finished. Laurie, I'm sorry for the night you've had, but you did well."

"Not good enough," I whisper. "Heather—"

"You did what you could. At least she has a chance."

I nod my agreement and sink into Aaron's arms.

"Dan, can I talk with you a minute?" Master Shane asks.

I watch as they walk to the reception area of the clinic. Master Shane is tall, at just over six foot, but Deputy Mansen towers over him. He's not just tall, he's burly. Master is incredibly fit and flexible from over four decades of martial arts. Dan Mansen, however, has the frame of a body builder from years of lifting weights. My mom says, with his big muscles and bald head, Deputy Mansen reminds her of Mr. Clean, without the earring. I've heard he has a nickname—Dan the Man. It fits him.

Mansen and Master are about the same age, and the rumor is, Mansen plans to retire next summer. Now…who knows?

While they're talking, I ask Aaron if he can try and find out if there's any news about Toby. He says he doesn't think there will be, but at my pleading look he finds the nurse. He was right, no news.

Within half an hour, Master Shane is driving us to Aaron's apartment. As we get close, things are different than the last time I was here.

"What's going on, Aaron?"

"Oh, this? I guess today, while we were at the clinic helping out, there was an incident here. You know my neighbor Bruno? His brother-in-law showed up with some guys and started breaking into a neighbor's apartment—someone who was gone when the attacks started. So Bruno and many of my other neighbors put together a neighborhood watch."

"His brother-in-law? A family member would do something like that?"

Aaron shrugs. "Seems he's got some issues."

"Issues?" Master scoffs. "That boy is trouble. He's been trouble for years—drugs, booze, theft, and in and out of county jail many times.

He almost went to the state pen once but managed a plea bargain. Trouble."

"And they've put up a blockade?" I motion to the two cars blocking the driveway into the complex, as Master Shane slows his truck. He waves his hand out the window and hollers, "Hey, there." A few seconds later one of the cars moves, unblocking the road.

After the car moves, Aaron says, "They thought it might help."

"Yeah, well, it might," Master Shane says. "But a couple of those idiots need to realize they're not trained for this sort of thing. They're going to get hurt or hurt someone they don't intend to. Dan's going to stop by here tomorrow, to give them some pointers."

"Deputy Mansen knows about this?" I ask.

"He does now. That's why I pulled him aside to talk before we left the clinic. I know these guys mean well, but..." He lets his voice fade away.

"Thanks for the ride, Bill," Aaron says.

"You bet. Hey, Laurie, Dan said you left your handgun in the nightstand when you went downstairs."

I can feel myself shrink, embarrassed I was so stupid. Not trusting my voice, I whisper, "Yes."

"We all need to start making a point to carry our weapons. You did well tonight with defending yourself up close and personal. But the truth is, you got lucky. They weren't armed; they were intoxicated, and they were stupid. You may be very proficient sparring on the mat, but if either of them would've had a gun, I think you know what would've happened."

"I'd be dead, sir," I respond, again in a whisper.

"You'd be dead," he agrees. "Aaron, this goes for you too. You both need to arm yourselves. Laurie lost her pistol in the fire. Do you have one for her?"

"I do, sir. She was using the 9-millimeter my dad trains all the kids on. I have my mom's .40 caliber in my gun safe. Laurie can use it. It's one of the guns she shot the first day we practiced at your place."

"You have a holster for her?"

"An inside the waistband holster."

Master gives me a quick glance. "You got clothes other than those shorts?"

"I have a few things she can wear," Aaron answers for me.

"Maybe we can ask around, find you a few other things. An IWB isn't going to work very well with shorts; they'll sag under the weight. And she'll never fit in your blue jeans."

"How about with sweats?" Aaron asks.

"Don't think so—same issue. I might have something she can use. Aaron, what I said to Laurie goes for you too."

"I'm armed now, sir. I've been carrying since the thing at the river."

"Got your bear gun?"

"Yes, sir, my Glock 20."

"Yeah, okay. Check in with me tomorrow. I want to know how you two are doing."

Chapter 26

When we get into Aaron's apartment, he opens the large east-facing front window. The sun is peeking over the Big Horn Mountains, bathing the living room in a pale-yellow glow. I sink into the sofa.

"Coffee?" Aaron asks. "Or would you like to sleep?"

"Coffee." After a long pause, I add, "Then sleep."

Aaron's kitchen range is electric, so he's using a camp stove for cooking. He takes it and a teakettle out the kitchen's sliding door to the patio. I lean back on the couch, trying not to think of anything. I close my eyes and see Jeremy's lifeless eyes. Squeezing my eyes tight, I try to clear my mind. I'm hit with an echoic memory—his head slamming into the hearth. I bolt upright and swallow hard, wondering if I'm going to vomit. My pounding heart makes it hard to regain control. In through my nose, out through my mouth.

I'm finally somewhat composed when Aaron returns with the steaming kettle. "Won't be long now," he says. "How about an energy bar to go with it?"

"Chocolate?"

Soon, he's sitting next to me while we drink coffee, share an apple, and eat our energy bars; chocolate for me, lemon for him.

After we're finished, Aaron leans forward. "I'm going over to the house. I'll relieve the people who have been monitoring the fire. After that, I'll help Thad at the firehouse. You should sleep while I'm gone."

"Finish telling me about Tabitha," I blurt, not even sure why I'm saying this now, at this time. Maybe I just want an excuse for him to stay a little longer, have him hold me and drive away the memories of death. Not just death—killing.

With a loud sigh, he settles into the couch. "Soon. Let me take care of these things. You get some sleep, then when I get back, we'll talk. You can have my room while you're here. I'll sleep on the couch. Let me change the sheets for you."

"I can do that," I say, feeling a little hurt he's putting me off.

"No, I'll do it. You just relax." He stands up and starts to walk away, but stops and says, "Are you okay being alone?"

"You mean while you go to the bedroom?" I try to give him a smile. Fluttering my fingers, I say, "I'm fine. You go do your stuff. You're right—I should sleep."

In addition to clean sheets, Aaron has put a pair of sweatpants and a T-shirt on the bed for me. I'm suddenly wishing we would've sent half of my clothes over here while we were sharing items. While I do have winter clothes belonging to his mom and sister here, I'm short on regular clothes. Fortunately, there are a few things in the backpack we put together the other day—a couple of tank tops, another pair of shorts, and a pair of underwear. Thankfully, I sleep in a light sports bra. I'd really be embarrassed if I didn't have *something* on underneath my shirt. I'm fortunate to have a pair of athletic shoes in the backpack Aaron put together for me—an old pair of his mom's, which fit surprisingly well—along with three pairs of nice hiking socks.

Aaron warns me to keep the bathroom door shut when I'm not using it. Even though the toilet still seems to function as it should, after adding water to the bowl to force a flush, there's a rank odor, like the sewer smell is seeping back up the pipes. I do what I have to do in the bathroom but move to the kitchen to brush my teeth and clean up as best I can. I save my cleaning water to rinse out the underclothes I'm wearing, hanging them to dry.

I toss and turn for a long time before finally falling into a restless sleep. When I wake up, I'm in the groggy state where I don't remember the things that happened. Then it all comes crashing back. *How's Heather? The house burned down. I killed Jeremy.*

I slip into Aaron's robe and go to the living room. The sun has shifted past the point of streaming in the east-facing window; it must be early afternoon. I slept much longer than I thought I would. I roll my head and then my shoulders. I need a workout.

I scrounge around the kitchen looking for a no-cook meal, finally settling on a spoonful of peanut butter and a handful of raisins. There's plenty of other food, but nothing that meets my current needs. And nothing that sounds very good right now.

Shortly after I finish my snack, Aaron returns. He gives me a quick kiss, then says, "You look like you got some rest. Feel better?"

I shrug. "A little. I still can't believe I killed someone."

He takes me into his arms, holding me while I cry.

Chapter 27

We make macaroni and cheese for a late lunch or early dinner—
whichever. Aaron has a small container of powdered creamer to use
in place of milk. It's the best mac and cheese I've ever had.

"I brought your car back," he says. "Glad you had that hide-a-key
in place. Since I'm supposed to only have one parking space, I took
my truck out to Master Shane's. I was able to get the utility trailer out
of my dad's shed earlier. Took me two trips, but I got things from the
shed and the yard that I thought we could use. I'm glad all of the
bicycles, dirt bikes, and winter sports gear were kept in the shed. Still,
the stuff we lost in the garage and house…"

While slurping down my macaroni, I bob my head.

"I think it's going to rain," he says. "After it does, we should be
able to salvage things from the house—some stuff anyway."

"The guns should be okay?"

He shrugs. "Probably not the one in your nightstand or the closet.
There were a couple still in the gun safe. The safe is fireproof, so those
should be okay. I have guns here, but I took several to Bill's place.
There's also a handgun stashed at our dojang."

"You took a handgun to our dojang? That seems so…" I search for
the right word, "disrespectful."

Mouth in a tight line, he shrugs.

"Okay. I understand." I nod. "How's the neighborhood watch
going?"

Aaron shakes his head. "Dan Mansen stopped by and talked to
them—gave them some pointers. Overall, he thinks it's a good idea.
There's been trouble in various parts of town. Starting tomorrow, I'm
taking a shift manning the roadblock."

"I can help too."

"I know you can. Maybe in a few days."

"Were you able to find out anything about Toby?"

"Nothing concrete. They can't find him on any lists of people
transferred to one of the other hospitals."

"What does that mean?"

"Right now, they don't know where he is."

"Is he assumed dead?"

"Not necessarily. He could've made it out of the hospital, and been taken in by someone, or is in one of the shelters. Prospect is in chaos right now, so it's hard to get information."

"How about Heather?"

"She made it to Billings. They had to take the back road. You know, the one by the state park? The main road was closed. Well, not exactly closed. Seems someone's now charging a toll to use it."

"A toll? I don't understand."

"Yeah, I don't really either. Some guys have it blocked off, and to drive on it, you have to give them food, water, or something they can use."

We finish our meal in silence. I can't believe people could just add a toll to a public road. How does that even work?

We use as little water as possible to clean the dishes. Even though Aaron had some water stored at his apartment, I'm glad the water we got at Master Shane's yesterday was left in the back of his truck. I completely forgot about it after we went to the clinic, but when I got up from my nap, the containers were sitting on the kitchen table. Aaron must have brought them in before he left this morning. At least we have water for the next several days.

"I'd like to make sure we have things organized so we can leave my apartment at a moment's notice," Aaron says.

"Okay? Organized how?"

"By having stuff we need, like the backpacks, in an easy-to-grab location. Maybe fill up a duffle bag or two with other things we think we can't live without. If a fire starts in this building, there's no way to stop it from spreading to each apartment."

I drop my eyes, not wanting to think about how quickly his parents' house burned down. And it's an older house, likely built more solid than these newer apartments. The space between houses in the Ogdens' neighborhood helped keep the fire from spreading; that and the diligence of the neighbors.

"Hey, Laurie, it wasn't your fault."

I nod. I want to agree with him, and in my mind, I know he's right, but I still feel some responsibility. What if I would've taken the handgun downstairs with me? I could've ended it before it started. Before Heather was hurt. Before the house burned down. Maybe I wouldn't have had to kill Jeremy and injure Chuck. Maybe just having the gun would've been enough to deter them.

Of course, one of the things Master Shane made a big deal about when giving us defensive training was using the gun and not just brandishing it—no waving it around to scare people. And if I'm going to shoot, I shoot to kill. I feel my body shudder.

Aaron puts his hand on my shoulder. "Should we get started?" Just then, we hear a clap of thunder in the distance. Aaron smiles. "Right on time."

The backpacks are stashed in the bedroom closet, ready to go. Aaron pulls out two duffle bags, old ones from Taekwondo with long straps to make it easy to sling them over a shoulder and wear messenger bag style.

We put food and water in one and clothes and medical supplies in the other. I think about all the food we lost in the house fire. Hopefully the basement was spared and some of the things downstairs can be salvaged.

"Oh! I almost forgot," Aaron says, "Master Shane told me to give you this."

He holds up a wide black neoprene strap. "Okay...I'm not sure what that is."

"Look." He undoes the Velcro, opening it up wide. "It's a belly band holster. He said he got it at a training thing and thought it'd work well under your workout clothes."

We spend several minutes figuring out how the belly band works. I like the way it fits, snug and comfortable around my waist. It's similar to a wide belt. Not only does it have options for carrying my pistol in a variety of positions, it also holds extra magazines. Aaron only has one extra mag for this gun, so it's easy to tuck it in.

Chapter 28

After the rain stops, we take my car to his parents' house. The house is still smoking, but there aren't any active flames. Parts of the house are still standing, and parts have collapsed. Where my bedroom was, above the living room, is gone. The back wall of the garage is still there, with the front opened up. Part of me is glad Aaron's parents are stuck in Wisconsin so they can't see what has become of their beautiful home. Maybe things will return to normal and we can rebuild it.

Does homeowner's insurance still exist? I've heard of small companies going out of business during localized events. With the tremendous destruction from these attacks, have all companies gone out of business? Of course, as far as I know, most of the attacks weren't against personal property, so maybe they haven't been affected. Does it really matter? There's no internet or phone to file a claim. What about mail?

Is the USPS still functioning? What is it they say? Something about working in rain, sleet, or snow? Not true in Wyoming. Our mail is often stopped due to blizzards. I can't imagine they're still functioning during this...whatever this is. Crisis? Catastrophe? Apocalypse? *Focus, Laurie.*

Straightening my shoulders, I ask, "Do you think it's safe to go inside?"

"Probably not," Aaron says.

We spend several minutes sitting in the car in silence, looking over the house. Crisis is a good word to use. Disaster is fine. Tragedy—it's definitely a tragedy. And catastrophe works, but not apocalypse. No, definitely not apocalypse. That just sounds too...final.

Aaron startles me when he says, "I'm going to check it out."

I open the door to follow him, but he says, "I'd rather you wait out here. Okay?"

I start to argue, then think better of it. Truthfully, I don't ever want to go in that house again. "Yeah. I'll wait. But don't be—don't do anything too risky."

"I'll be careful." He gives me a quick kiss, then makes his way into the garage. A few minutes later, he comes out carrying a plastic tote. The edges are melted and the lid is missing.

"What'd you find?"

"There were clothes in the dryer."

"Clothes in the dryer? Oh! I completely forgot I was doing laundry before the cyberattacks. I never even thought to go back for my stuff. Were there clothes in the washing machine too?"

"I didn't look there. You've had clothes in the washing machine since Saturday?"

I manage to look sheepish as I say, "Maybe. Um, maybe since Friday."

Aaron smiles and shakes his head. "Let me go check. There's a few other things too. Here, I'll need to use the tote."

I take the clothes out of the tote and spread them on the hood. I'll fold them while Aaron goes back in. Pajamas, underwear, two more sports bras, and several sets of workout clothes. They do smell a little smoky, but none are damaged. Maybe, if I hang them outside on Aaron's patio, they'll air out.

If I remember right, the washing machine has jeans and T-shirts. Is there any chance one of my doboks survived the fire? I had one in the laundry basket next to the washing machine. I can't imagine it did; the laundry basket was made of wicker.

Aaron returns with the still barely wet, slightly mildewed smelling clothes. I make a face; the combination of mildew and smoke is not pleasant. They'll need more than an airing out. Will I be able to get rid of that smell and wear these clothes?

"The door to the half bath was shut. The fire didn't reach in there," he says, as he empties the mildewed clothes on the car hood. "The stuff on the counters was scorched, but there's towels, washcloths, and even toilet paper in the cabinets. It all looks fine."

"Toilet paper survived a fire? How's that possible?"

"I don't know. I guess, since the door was closed and it's an interior room, there wasn't enough oxygen to burn it? The roll that was on the holder is gone and things were melted from the heat, but inside the cabinets..." He shrugs. "I can't explain it."

"Maybe more stuff survived the fire? Right?"

He gives me a small smile and a nod as he heads in for another load. With the front of the garage gone, I watch as he pokes around. He spends a lot of time in there, but when he comes back out, he doesn't have much to show for it. The garage didn't fare very well in the fire.

"Okay, I'm going to see about getting into the basement," he says. "Are the stairs still intact?"

"I didn't move that far into the house to find out. I looked into the kitchen from the laundry room but didn't go inside."

"Is it safe?"

He shrugs. "No, probably not."

"So don't do it then. Let's just take what we have."

"Let me at least look. I want to check the pantry too. If the door was shut, maybe it wasn't destroyed. Maybe it will be like the bathroom and we can save some of the food."

I shake my head. I know he's going to do what he wants to do. "Be safe," I mutter, then watch him go back inside the house. When he returns a few minutes later, he's smiling.

"The pantry door was shut. The rice and stuff like that didn't make it, but there's canned goods. Most of the labels are charred. Some we can't read, but I think the cans are still okay to eat. A few were bulging. Those aren't okay, so I left them."

"Did you get them all?"

"Yeah, everything we could save. And I took a look at the basement stairs. They were made out of wood and most are gone. I'll need to bring back a ladder to get down there. That was one of the things I took to Bill's earlier today. We'll do that tomorrow—give everything a little longer to cool off. It's still pretty warm in the kitchen area, lots of lingering smoke too."

"So that's it for today?"

"Yep. I was thinking we should go to Bill's place. We can wash your clothes there."

"His washing machine works?"

"Probably, if the generator is running. But even if it's not, he has plenty of water, so we can wash them by hand. Unless you'd prefer a rock on the river?"

"Ha. No thanks. Let's try Master Shane's."

Chapter 29

Master Shane's generator isn't large enough to power his washing machine. And since it's getting late in the day, we decide we'll come back tomorrow to hand wash my clothes and hang them to dry. What's another day for my stinky wet clothes?

"Mind if we leave the rest of the stuff also?" I ask. "It's all pretty smoky. Maybe a night on your porch will air them out."

"Sure, that's fine. I doubt the area wildlife will bother them."

I smile at a memory of a raccoon getting into Master's cooler once. He'd left it outside instead of bringing it in after a day of fishing. The raccoon loved the leftover sandwiches. While Master Shane's property isn't directly on the river, he's less than half a mile away—close enough to have raccoons and other water-loving wildlife visit regularly.

Aaron and I stay only a few minutes longer. Even with my nap earlier, I'm tired and ready for bed.

At the apartment, I clean up while Aaron makes us a snack—tuna fish and crackers, with no mayo in the tuna. That was at my place with the generator keeping it cool. At least the generator was spared. Since it sat outside, it wasn't burned, and is in the utility trailer at Master Shane's.

After eating, we sit on the couch. Before the *crisis*, we didn't sit alone on the couch—one of the things I grumped about. Now, even though I'm enjoying sitting here next to the man I love, I'd give anything to have things the way they were.

Before the planes crashed, before the power went out, *before I killed Jeremy*. I squeeze my eyes tight, attempting to hold back my tears. After several minutes, I feel myself calming.

I'm just about to tell Aaron I'm going to go to bed, when he takes my hand and says, "I'd like to finish telling you about Tabitha."

"All right," I say, turning so I can somewhat face him. I slip off my shoes and pull my feet up, making myself comfortable.

He gives me a small smile. "I've been afraid of being this close to you. While I know we're both adults and can control our urges, I was afraid it'd remind me of when I didn't control myself."

I start to speak, to tell him he shouldn't think of himself that way, but he shakes his head and says, "I have to say these things. It's important you know."

"Okay, Aaron." I nod and motion locking my lips and throwing away the key so he knows I'll try to stay quiet.

He gives me a tight, amused smile and a shake of his head, which I interpret as, *what am I going to do with you?*

Chapter 30

He immediately sobers. "I truly thought I loved Tabitha. I thought she loved me. I thought we'd get married—not in the way we did, but because of love. I understand now why it's important to wait until marriage. God's plan for marriage is perfect and right. I wish we wouldn't have rushed it. But even so, there are things I'll always cherish."

He takes a deep breath. "After dinner that night, after we'd spent the day at the hospital thinking our baby was dying, Tabitha went back into the bedroom. She slammed the door so hard a painting her folks gave us fell off the wall. I was putting it back up when she came out of the room, suitcase in hand.

"She raised her other hand in a stopping motion, telling me to keep quiet, I guess. She said, 'For a few minutes today, I was happier than I've been in months. I felt like there was a light at the end of the tunnel, like I could breathe again. Those few minutes were during the time Dr. Mathews was preparing us for the death of the baby.'"

Aaron closes his eyes for a long moment. "I was dumbfounded. I knew she wasn't happy, but I didn't realize…I felt like such an idiot. I tried to tell her how sorry I was, how I could do better—be a better husband. She laughed. Not a nice laugh, but one full of anger, or maybe venom. I don't know, but it wasn't a pleasant sound. Then she said, 'I don't want a husband. I don't want a baby. I'm leaving. I don't care what my dad says, we're getting a divorce. When it's born, you can come and get it.'

"'Him,' I corrected her. I had to make sure she remembered our baby was a boy. 'Whatever,' she said, flicking her wrist. 'Boy, girl. Doesn't matter. I want out. *He* is all yours.' I nodded numbly and said, 'No problem. Call when it's time. I'll be there.' Nope. Not what she wanted. She said she'd call me after he was born. She didn't want me there for it. She didn't want to see me at all."

Aaron's hanging his head, staring into his lap. I watch as a tear hits his thigh, making a dark spot on his jeans. I want to hold him, say something to comfort him. But I restrain myself and let him finish.

"And then she left," he says. "She took the Mustang her parents bought her for graduation. She floored it on the way out, leaving tire marks in the driveway and more when she pulled into the street. I was confused, hurt, sad, and—if I'm honest—a little relieved. We were miserable.

"I did the dishes, cleaned up the kitchen, did a short workout, and then watched some TV. I thought about calling my parents, but what would I tell them? My wife of less than a month left me? She'll call when she delivers? I wasn't up to that.

"A short while later, there was a knock on the door. It was Bill Shane in full uniform. He only had a little over a week until retirement. At first, I thought he was off shift and visiting. I quickly realized that wasn't the case."

Chapter 31

Aaron looks up at me, meeting my eyes. "I know you've heard the rumors, but I need to make sure you know what really happened."

I nod, as he says, "Tabitha was in a car accident. She was on Highway 120 between Prospect and Cody, going over Skull Creek Hill. Bill knew it was bad. She was critical and taken by life flight to Billings. Bill was ending his shift early and would drive me there. Deputy Dan Mansen was notifying Tabitha's parents, and said he'd tell my parents, too, if I'd like.

"By the time we got to the hospital, Tabitha was clinically dead, with her heart beating only because of the machines. Our baby was still alive, and they were waiting for my decision of what to do. Her parents showed up a few minutes later. That was pretty terrible. I was glad Bill was with me. I realized that night what a true friend he is. Not just a teacher, a real friend."

I touch his arm. I'd heard from Aaron's sister that Master Shane intervened when Tabitha's dad threatened to beat the tar out of Aaron. At the time, I had a hard time imagining Tabitha's extremely overweight and out of shape dad getting the best of Aaron. But after thinking about it, I suspect Aaron wouldn't have even tried to fight back. He would've understood her dad was in anguish and lashing out.

"I decided to try and save our child," Aaron says. "She may not have wanted him, not wanted to be a mom, but he was still alive. And I loved him. With every fiber of my being, I loved our son. That's probably what got tongues wagging the most. I know Monica Daniels enjoyed telling people I thought of Tabitha as an incubator and nothing more."

Yes, that was one of the things she said about Aaron. She had several other stories too, including Tabitha had deliberately drove off the road, killing herself. Of course, according to Mrs. Daniels, Aaron drove Tabby to suicide.

Another rumor was Aaron drugged her and staged the accident, managing to drive home and pretend like he'd been there the whole night. That one actually gained enough traction that there was an investigation to prove Aaron was home. Thankfully, cameras on the four traffic lights Tabitha drove through on her way through Wesley, plus three more in Prospect, all showed her alone in the car. Her stop for food at the McDonalds in Prospect also helped.

"Two days later, Tabitha started bleeding and went into labor. We wanted to keep the baby inside as long as possible. They gave Tabitha some shots to mature his lungs and thought, even though he was premature, he was old enough to survive. Dr. Mathews said she was twenty-five weeks, two days, when we went in for our appointment. A micro-preemie, the nurse said, but with medical intervention, micro-preemies have a good chance.

"They allowed me in the delivery room. And at first, I thought everything was fine. He was small, but he let out a little cry. Not really a cry, more of a whimper or a mewl, like a kitten. Then something happened and things went crazy. Someone yelled, 'He's crashing!' I moved to the corner. I could see what was happening, but just barely. They worked on him, putting all kinds of tubes and things in, but...you know the rest."

I do know the rest. They couldn't save him. The theory was he was injured in the accident. They'd done ultrasounds and nothing showed up. But he had some bruising on his back and the back of his head.

Aaron sighs. "They removed the tubes and put us in a room so I could hold him. He was so small. My wedding band fit around his arm like a giant bracelet. A special photographer came by and took photos of him. Of us—of Adam and me."

One of the photos is sitting on the coffee table, next to the couch we're sitting on. His parents display Adam's picture with the other grandkids' pictures. Adam looks so perfect and peaceful, like he's sleeping. Aaron has Adam's pictures not only around his house but also in his wallet. In one of the photos, Aaron looks so sad but also proud— a father holding the son he loves.

Chapter 32

I pull Aaron into my arms and hold him as he cries. It's been two years since Adam died, but I know not a day goes by Aaron doesn't think of him. It was almost a year after Adam's death when we started seeing each other.

Yeah, you can imagine how that really got Monica Daniels, and others like her, talking. It wasn't like we planned to date. We were friends, like we'd been for so many years. Then, one day, I realized my love for Aaron had changed.

He was no longer my little brother. Aaron was an amazing man. He'd had tremendous heartache but was making his way back from it. Finding his new church and really focusing on God was a big part of it. At first, Aaron compared himself to King David. He thought he'd caused Adam's death by being with Tabitha before they were married. He struggled with the guilt for a long time. Finally, Pastor Robert helped him realize guilt is part of bereavement.

"I can't risk something like that again, Laurie," Aaron says, straightening and looking into my eyes. "A part of me died when Adam died. We'll do things right—honorably. I now understand my sin didn't cause Adam's death. I don't care what other people think of me, only what you and God think. Keeping our relationship pure until we're married is something I have to do...something we have to do."

"Of course, Aaron. You know I've always understood that. I respect your decision and agree we need to wait. Even though I'm living here now, that won't change anything."

"But it does, Laurie. These last few days have changed everything. I've made many promises," he drops his head and whispers, "promises I don't think I can keep."

Chapter 33

Aaron takes me in his arms. "I don't think I can keep the promise I made to your parents, the promise to wait until they return from India to marry you."

I can't help but smile. With things falling apart around us, I've tried not thinking about how I want to be his wife.

"What are you saying?"

"At the moment, not much." He gives a small laugh. "But soon, I'm going to be saying a lot more. I love you. Now, let's get to bed."

I waggle my eyebrows at him.

He shakes his head and wags his finger playfully. "What *am* I going to do with you? That's not what I mean. You have the bed; I have the couch."

As tired as I am, once again I'm tossing and turning—thinking about Aaron, Heather, the house burning down, and killing Jeremy.

I let out a big sigh then try fixing my pillow. Just as I get comfortable, a huge boom shakes the windows. I bolt up in bed and start toward the window. At the sound of gunfire, I throw myself on the floor.

I crawl away from the window and toward the living room. "Aaron? Aaron!"

"I'm here," he yells back, also crawling on the floor, meeting me in the hallway.

"What's happening?"

"I don't know. I guess the guys at the roadblock have trouble."

"Do they have explosives?"

"Not that I know of."

"But wasn't that a bomb or something?" I can hear myself freaking out, my voice in a high whine.

"I don't know, Laurie," Aaron answers. As always, his voice is calm and collected.

"What should we do? Help them?"

"Stay here. The hallway should be safe from the shooting. I'm going to grab our backpacks and duffle bags."

119

"Are we leaving?"

"We'll get ready, in case we need to. I'll grab the rifles out of my gun safe too. Where's your pistol?"

I hesitate to answer. Once again, I've left it behind. "It's on the nightstand, in the holster. Can you grab my clothes off the chair? My shoes are underneath." It's then I notice Aaron's fully dressed; he's even wearing his work boots.

"How'd you get dressed so fast?"

"I didn't undress." He shrugs.

"The shooting has stopped," I say.

"Good. Be right back."

Before he comes back, there's another explosion followed by more shooting. I let out a yelp when I hear glass break. "Aaron!"

"I'm okay," he says, poking his head out the door. "I think it was the living room window. I have the rifles." He scoots them along the carpet, followed by two boxes of bullets. Cartridges—Master Shane calls them cartridges or ammunition, not bullets. My mind is in chaos, focusing on trivial details.

Aaron slides back into the bedroom. "What are you doing?" I hiss.

"Getting your stuff."

He's back in a minute, handing me my sweats, T-shirt, socks, and shoes. He sits my sidearm on the floor. "Can you just put these on over your shorts?"

"Yes, just give me a minute."

He slides open the hall closet and pulls out our bags. I dress as quickly as I can, slipping on the belly band holster before sliding the sweats on over my shorts. The shooting is still sporadic.

Aaron stands at the edge of the hall, rifle in hand. He's wearing his backpack and has the heavier of the two duffel bags by his foot.

I put my backpack on. "Okay, I'm ready. What are we doing?"

"I'm going to try and see what's happening. This—" he motions to the rifle leaning against the wall, "—is the .22 you've shot before. It's pretty light and has a long, single-point sling. See?" He lifts it up. "You can wear it over the backpack. You should still be able to carry the duffle. Wear it like a messenger bag, with the duffle hitting your left hip. It shouldn't be in the way of the rifle."

"Okay. Where are we going?" I lean out of the hallway, slightly looking toward the front door. There's a kitchen chair wedged underneath the doorknob. I'm glad Aaron thought to do that. It's dark, and I can't tell for certain if the window was hit in the shooting spree.

"Sounds like the shooting is coming from the parking lot. We're probably safe here. But if we need to, we'll leave through the slider."

"Good thing you're on the ground floor."

"Yeah. Except, if I was on the second floor, the window might not have been shot out."

"Good point." I check the rifle.

"It's loaded but none in the barrel. Go ahead and make it ready. The magazine holds five. The ammunition holder on the stock has another five. I put the box in the outside pocket of your backpack."

I thought the pack felt heavier than before.

"You okay, Laurie? You ready in case we have to move fast? Drop the duffle if you can't handle it. We can make do without it."

"I'm ready."

Aaron stoops down, making his way to the window. We haven't heard shooting in the last minute or so. This isn't a huge apartment complex; there are three buildings with a total of twenty apartments— mostly singles or couples around our age, but there's a couple of families. I hope no one has been hurt—or worse. I think of Jeremy and his lifeless eyes.

Aaron's no sooner at the window when another shot rings out, followed by a volley of several. He drops to the floor and crawls back.

"Yeah, we'll need to go out the back. Let's just relax and wait for a bit."

"What'd you see?"

"Not much. A couple of guys walking around. I only caught a glimpse."

"Who was it?"

"Don't know. I didn't recognize them, but with the lack of light and only a quick look, it could've been anyone."

We stay put at the edge of the hallway for many minutes. The shooting has stopped, and there haven't been any recent explosions. I'm starting to think maybe it's over.

"What's that noise?" I ask.

Aaron screws up his face. "Crying?"

Oh, yeah. As much crying as I've been doing lately, you'd think I'd recognize it.

Suddenly, the shooting resumes. This time, it sounds like it's right outside our apartment. I grab Aaron's arm. "Too close," he whispers.

There's a crash, then a loud yell, followed by several quick shotgun blasts.

"Was that in the apartment next door?" I ask, barely above a whisper.

Another boom from the shotgun—a woman screams, followed by another shot.

"Let's go, Laurie. Out the back. I'll go out first and make sure it's clear, then cover you while you run for the shrubs along the edge of the property."

"Cover me? How do you know how to do that?"

"I don't! But let's pretend I do so we can get out of here."

"Why don't we just stay and shoot them if they come in?"

"We don't know who it is or how many there are. Getting out and running away is our best option."

"What about your neighbors?"

"Laurie. You are my concern. We need to go. *Now.*"

Chapter 34

We scoot into the kitchen, staying low, and then hide behind the cabinet.

"All right, I'm going to open the door and step out. I'll come back for you when I know it's clear."

"Aaron." I grab his arm. "Be careful."

He leans toward me and gives me a hard kiss. "I love you, Laurie."

He starts to pull away, but I raise my hand to his cheek, giving it a quick caress. He needs a shave. His eyes reflect his love for me but also something more—fear.

"Are you sure?" I ask. "This is the best thing to do?"

Just then, there's a loud bang on the door. Someone's trying to kick it in.

"Let's go," he says in a loud whisper, already moving. "Stay behind me and stay low."

Thankfully, the patio door isn't visible from the living room. If they gain entry, hopefully they won't see us. Aaron has the slider barely open when the loud crack of the wooden front door announces the breach.

Aaron drops to the ground and motions me to move. I'm right behind him, stumbling onto the patio. As soon as I'm out, he slides the door shut.

"Stay low," he hisses, rifle at the ready. I'm amazed at how he's balancing everything.

I try to mimic him, holding the plinking rifle at hip level, safety off with my finger outside the trigger guard. My heart is pounding as I try to remember gun safety; I don't want to accidentally shoot Aaron...or myself.

We're moving quick, doing essentially a duck walk, something we've become proficient at through training.

We finally make it to the dense shrubs along the edge of the property. I'm breathing hard—much harder than I should be from this small amount of exertion. We're in the shrubs enough to be well hidden but still have a partial view of the buildings.

"You okay?" Aaron asks in a low voice. There's sporadic shooting and another explosion.

"I-I c-can't catch m-my breath."

"Probably the fear. We'll be okay. Focus on your breathing."

"W-why are they doing t-this?"

He shakes his head, watching the apartment complex.

"Are we s-safe here?"

"I'm not sure. We should probably keep moving, get away from here."

"Go w-where?"

"Catch your breath, then we'll decide. Stay back and don't shake the branches."

I nod my agreement, then realize it's dark and he isn't looking at me anyway. "Okay. Where's the cops?" I whisper.

"I don't know. Without 911 to call, I guess they'd either have to hear the shooting and explosions—"

"They should hear them as loud as it is," I interject.

"Maybe," he agrees.

A figure walks around the edge of the building. He's holding his weapon to his eye, using the scope as a monocular. I shrink back slightly as Aaron says, "Shh."

The guy spends several minutes scoping the area. At one point, I think he sees us when he stiffens and drops to one knee.

"Should we run?" I whisper. Then the guy stands up and walks back around the apartment building. I let out my breath.

"I can't be sure, but I think that's the guy who shot at me," Aaron says.

"Just now?"

"What?"

"Shot at us just now? Oh! You mean on the river?"

"Right. I think it was him. There isn't enough moonlight for me to be sure."

"I don't...why? That makes no sense."

"Maybe they got tired of camping and decided to find something else."

"An apartment complex? Why not take over one of those new subdivisions on the other side of town? Those places are nice."

"I don't know, Laurie. I don't know why they're here or what they want. All I know is there have been explosions and gunshots. From

124

the sounds of things, my next-door neighbor and his wife may have been killed. We need to get out of here and find someplace safe." While his voice mostly has its usual calmness and control, there's an edge to it.

I stay quiet, feeling properly reprimanded. I didn't even think he might be feeling bad about his friend.

After a minute, he says, "Let's go to the dojang. We can stay there tonight."

"Can we get to my car?"

"Not a chance. We'll need to walk. It's only five blocks."

I agree it's not far, but with the backpack, duffle bag, and guns, I'm weighed down.

"You ready?" Aaron asks.

Chapter 35

We don't have any trouble reaching the dojang. To be safe, we traveled by moonlight only, not using a flashlight. We go in the back door, locking it behind us, and Aaron puts a chair under the knob before he turns on a flashlight. Not his little keychain light, but a larger LED light.

"Let's use the ladies' locker room," he says.

"Good idea. It smells better than the men's."

"Not just that. It's an interior room to give us a little more protection."

"We weren't followed?" I try to make it a statement but it comes out more of a question.

"No, but things are so crazy right now, I'd just feel better if you had a little more protection," he says, while we move to the locker room. I'm wrong. It doesn't smell better. Like Aaron's bathroom, there's an odor wafting up the sewer pipes and escaping through the toilets.

"We."

"What?"

"We will have a little more protection."

He steps into the locker room, flashing his light all around. Our dressing area is at the front, with a row of a dozen small lockers and a shelving unit for stashing workout bags. This section is covered in industrial carpet; then there's a tiled section with two toilets and three sinks. Past that are two private showers and two curtained dressing areas. The men's locker room has the same layout, except it has three high windows in the locker section.

"Anything we can do about the smell?" I ask, as Aaron begins unloading his gear.

I follow suit. I start to unzip my backpack when he says, "Let's leave everything as is, in case we need to move again. You have clothes in your locker?"

I nod.

"You can change into those if you want."

126

I think about it, *do I want to?* What's in the locker is pretty much what I'm wearing now. I have yoga pants, a shirt, a couple pairs of socks, a pair of shoes, a dobok, assorted toiletries, basic first aid equipment—for those inevitable cuts and such from a hard workout—shower shoes, and a few snacks. "I think I'll just take off what I slipped over the top of my sleeping clothes and call it good."

Aaron nods. "I don't know what we can do about the smell. At least it isn't as bad as my apartment."

"It's not great," I mutter.

"I'll grab a couple of blankets from the office." He hands me his small keychain flashlight. "I'll be right back."

I shine the light around the room, looking at nothing in particular. I should be crying and completely distraught over tonight's events. Instead, I'm almost numb. I think of the scream from Aaron's neighbor—what's her name? Jennifer? Gina? I can't remember, but her scream was followed by the blast of a gun. That was terrible. Why am I not more upset?

And those guys seemed like they would've happily shot us too. They broke into Aaron's apartment. They're probably eating our food and drinking our water. Could it be like Aaron said? Did they just get tired of living on the river—assuming it was the same guy he saw from the river—and they wanted a roof over their head and comfortable beds to sleep in? They were willing to kill for a bed?

I can feel the heat rising up my face. I'm still not feeling distraught; now I'm mad. Mad anyone could have such little regard for another human that they're willing to kill for…for what?

Aaron walks back into the room, catching me fully in the eyes with the flashlight. "Thanks a lot," I snap.

"Whoa. Sorry, Laurie. It wasn't on purpose."

I close my eyes and drop my head. "Sorry," I whisper.

"It's okay." He drops the blankets in a chair and takes me into his arms.

I don't cry, even though I want to. I'd probably feel better if I did. After a minute, I ask, "Can we sleep?"

"Yeah. I found a couple of blankets and a pillow in our first aid stash. Let's make you a bed."

"Stay in here with me, Aaron."

"I'm going to run over to the sheriff substation first. Then I'll sleep in here."

What? No. He can't leave me here alone.

"Don't go."

"I have to. What if they don't know what's happening? It's not far. I'll be back in about twenty minutes."

I think about where it is from here—less than half a mile. Aaron can jog that in a few minutes. "Okay, but I'm not sleeping until you get back."

"Good idea. I want you to put the chair back in place after I leave. You'll need to move it so I can get back in."

"Can we put a chair at the front door too?"

"I already did." He spreads out the thicker of the two blankets on the floor.

"I'll take care of this, Aaron. Go, so you can get back quickly."

He leaves the duffle bag with me but straps his backpack on. "Just in case," he says. He's still wearing his sidearm and slings the rifle over his shoulder. "Okay. Lock it up behind me. I'll knock when I get back."

"Like a code or something?"

He gives me a weird look. "You'll know it's me."

As soon as he's out the door, I reposition the chair. I walk around for a few minutes, checking out the dojang in the dark. Even though the front windows are boarded up, I'm careful not to flash my light around too much, for fear of being discovered. I'm near the front of the building when I'm suddenly so tired I'm sure I'll collapse. I can barely make my legs carry me to the locker room section.

I crumple into a chair in the hallway. It's hard plastic, and not at all comfortable, but it doesn't matter at the moment. I don't even try and keep track of time. I simply sit in the chair.

There's a light knock on the door. *Dit, dit, dit, dah, dah, dah, dit, dit, dit.* I give a small smile. I'd almost forgotten about the year Aaron was learning Morse code. He wanted to be a fighter pilot and was convinced all fighter pilots must know Morse code. How old was he? Thirteen?

I remove the chair and start to unlock the door. I stop suddenly. *What if it's not him?* Anyone can tap on a door. I can't even remember any of the Morse alphabet, so I don't know what he tapped out.

"Laurie, it's me," the whisper carries through the door, as I watch the deadbolt turn. He's using his key; of course it's him.

"Hey," I say, opening the door a crack.

"Hey, yourself." He gives me his cute smile; the smile doesn't reach his eyes.

"Were you able to report it?"

"They already knew."

"Oh, good. Do they have everything under control? Can we go home?"

He frowns and shakes his head. "Not yet. We'll stay here for now. They aren't really able to do much. I guess there are a few more deputies coming in from Prospect as soon as it's light. They'll take care of it then."

"They aren't going to help tonight?"

"They can't do it, Laurie."

"Was Monica Daniels there again? Was she—"

"It wasn't her. It was Bill's friend, the jailer. We've met him at a few cookouts, but I can't remember his name and was too embarrassed to ask."

"Old squinty eye?" I ask, unable to remember his real name either. He's a nice guy, but one eye is always partially closed. I asked Master Shane about it before, and he said he doesn't think it's a medical issue but rather a habit.

"Yes, that one. Let's get some sleep."

Chapter 36

I wake to the smell of coffee. I'm instantly transported to memories of my dad and feeling safe in his presence. But Dad isn't here; he's on the other side of the world in India. I'm glad he and Mom are living their dream, but I wish they were here with me. Even though being with Aaron during this time is wonderful, I need my parents.

"Are you awake?" Aaron whispers.

"Yes, barely. The coffee smells good."

"It's the instant kind from the individual packets. I only have one titanium cup with my camp stove. You mind if we share?" He kneels next to me.

"I don't mind, but will we be sharing only one cup or two cups?" I try to look stern and fail.

"Oh, we'll share two cups for sure. Don't worry, we'll get enough caffeine in you." He smiles, offering me the cup. I sit up, leaning against the wall. Aaron has already folded up the other blanket. We both slept in the women's locker room last night—with a good six feet between us.

I take a sip. He's right, it's good. Very robust. "Yum, I might just keep this all for myself."

"Hey, now," he chastises, sitting by my side.

Without speaking, we take turns sipping from the cup. I offer him the last swallow, not to be nice but because, just like my dad, I don't drink to the bottom of the cup.

"I'll get us another cup," Aaron says.

"Sounds good. While you're doing that, I'm going to use the bathroom."

"Okay, there's several cases of water in the office. I'll grab a couple in case you need to flush."

"No, that's fine. I won't need to flush. Just stay out of here for a few minutes." I start to shoo him away, but then rethink it. "You know, I will take some water so I can wash my face and brush my teeth." I reach for my backpack and pull out the little travel-sized toothbrush and toothpaste. I'm very grateful Aaron insisted on setting up two backpacks for each of us. My other one was in the house when it caught fire, but this one is a well-stocked duplicate.

After a second cup of coffee and granola bars from the dojang's stash, Aaron says, "Let's walk over to the sheriff substation and see what the situation is."

"Okay. Let me fold up my blankets. Should I put them back in the office?"

"Yeah. Let's do that."

After we get everything straightened up, we put our packs on. "We'll leave the duffle bags here," Aaron says. "I don't want to carry them unless we have to. Last night, we were way too loaded. It was dumb on my part to think we could handle as much as we did."

I nod my agreement—not that he's dumb, but that I want to leave the duffle bags. We *were* carrying way too much last night. "The rifles?" I ask.

Aaron hesitates. "Leave them. I feel strange about walking around with them during the daylight. We can stash them in my locker. You have your gun on you?"

I lift my shirt slightly to show off the belly band.

He nods. "Let's go then."

We don't see anyone for the first several blocks. Traffic, both driving and walking, increases as we near the substation. At the sheriff substation, there are at least a dozen people milling around outside. We say hello to several we recognize.

A boy who's about sixteen years old stops Aaron. "Dude, was that your apartment complex hit last night?"

Aaron answers with a nod.

"Man! That sucks. You two are okay, though? You got away."

"Yeah, we're okay."

"How'd you hear about it?" I ask.

"Are you kidding? Everyone knows. Heard they killed a lot of people and are holding others hostage. Sheriff and the city po-po are there now, trying to negotiate a surrender or something."

I can feel myself pale as the night with Jeremy and Chuck rushes back. "They're holding people hostage?"

Aaron reaches for my hand. "So it's not settled yet?"

"Not even close, dude."

Aaron nods and turns to me. "We probably have the info we need for now."

131

"Yeah," I agree.

"Hey, man, did you hear about the assassination?"

Aaron and I share a look. More terrorist attacks? I haven't even listened to the radio since the day the hospital in Prospect caught fire. I have no idea what's happening.

We both shake our head.

"Yeah, dude, one of the deputy sheriffs."

"Our sheriff deputies?" I gasp.

"Yep, right."

"Who?" Aaron asks.

"The big bald one."

"Oh no," I cry.

"Deputy Mansen?" Aaron asks.

"Yeah, maybe. They call him Dan the Man."

I shake my head as tears flow down my cheeks. Aaron clears his throat several times before asking, "What happened?"

He shrugs and says, so nonchalantly I want to punch him in the nose, "Someone broke into his house and killed him. Rumor is, it was some dude from his past who had a beef with him."

"They get the guy?" Aaron asks.

"Don't think so." He raises his palms and shrugs. "Of course, you know how gossip goes in this town."

Aaron nods. "Yeah. I do."

The kid we're talking to waves across the parking lot to someone. "Hey, guys, see you later. Sorry about your place."

Aaron and I stand there for many minutes, silent and unmoving. Finally, I say, "Do you think Master Shane has heard?"

"Let's go inside. Maybe whoever is manning the desk will have more info."

"What if it's...what did Master call her? Secretary Ratched?"

"If it's Mrs. Daniels, we'll just leave." Aaron nods grimly.

132

Chapter 37

There are lots of people inside, but they aren't lined up at the desk. More like just hanging out, waiting. It's not Monica Daniels at the desk, but rather the jailer Aaron described last night. I still can't remember his name.

We hustle up to the desk. He looks at us with worn tired eyes; the one usually in a squint is almost fully closed, the other not far behind. *Can he even see?*

In the dim light, I have to squint to read his nametag. B. Wyatt. That's right! Brandt. Brandt Wyatt. He's been a guest, along with Deputy Mansen and several others, at many of Master Shane's barbecues.

"Oh, hey, Aaron," he says, his eyes opening up slightly. "Things are still a mess at your place. Not sure when we'll get it under control so you can go home."

"Yes, we heard. No problem. I just hope everyone's safe." A look of utter despair crosses Brandt's face. Aaron lowers his voice. "I heard about Dan Mansen. Is it true?"

Wyatt lowers his eyes and mutters, "It's true."

"Does Bill know?"

Brandt shrugs. "I put it out over the radio for him to come in. I didn't mention what happened, just asked him to report. He told me the other day he's monitoring with an old police scanner. Let me try again."

He sends out a totally benign message, asking former deputy Shane to report to the substation at his earliest convenience.

"Have you heard some people's phones are working?" Brandt asks.

"What? No! That's great," I say, wondering if my phone will work. *Where is my phone? Was it in the house when it caught fire?* No. It's in my car. I had it out there on the charger. I guess it's still there. "What about the electricity? Is it back?"

"Not yet."

"Are you sure?" I ask, trying not to sound completely deflated.

"Sorry—I'm sure. I have the light over this desk switched on so I'll know immediately."

"But the phones are working?" Aaron asks.

"Yep. Not reliably. I've tried mine a few times. I haven't been able to get it to work. But we had someone in here earlier who was able to reach their family in Washington State or somewhere."

"Maybe we can reach our parents," I say to Aaron, touching his arm.

Aaron nods. "Can you try Bill on your phone? Do you have his number?"

"Yep. I'll try."

"If you reach him or he shows up, can you pass on a message to him?" Aaron asks.

"Sure." Brandt nods. "No problem."

"Ask him to stop by the dojang. Tell him about my apartment if you want."

"Sure, Aaron, I'll do it."

"When are you off?" I ask.

"Who knows? We don't have anyone else to cover the desk."

I can't help but ask, "What about Monica Daniels?"

"You haven't heard?"

The way he says it, my blood runs cold. Tentatively, I shake my head.

"She's dead, murder-suicide."

I'm shocked. I know her husband. While she was a gossip monger, he was always quiet and kind. More than once I've heard him whisper *enough* when she'd exceed what he considered common decency. My dad and him were still friends when Dad left for India. Mr. Daniels was even at their going away party—not Monica. She wasn't there and made many comments afterward about what a disgusting show it was with my folks acting all hoity-toity since they're now missionaries.

"I can't believe Mr. Daniels would do that," I say.

"He didn't! She did."

"What?" Aaron exclaims.

"Yep. She called from her radio requesting assistance. By the time we got there... anyway. She's not the only one. You know the Riverstone family?"

We both nod; they were members of our old church.

134

"Yeah, all dead. Mom and dad killed the kids and then themselves. I guess people think things are going to get worse before they get better, and they don't want to deal."

My breath completely leaves me. I saw her in the grocery store a few weeks ago, before the terrorist attacks started, with her three children. The youngest was only two, and she told me she was expecting again.

"I don't understand. Why? Why would they do that?"

Brandt gives me a long hard look. In a very low, monotone voice, he says, "Don't you know what's happening?"

I must have given him a blank look because he says, "James Riverstone understood what we're facing. You know he was in Afghanistan? He'd seen stuff. Too much stuff. He didn't want his wife and children to be subjected to the horror he thinks is coming."

"I-I...she was so nice," I say in a whisper.

"That she was. That she was," Brandt says.

"We have a couple of friends we're wondering about," Aaron says. "Toby James. He was injured several days ago and taken to Prospect before the fire. Would you know if he's been located yet?"

"Sorry, you'll want to check at the clinic on that."

"And another girl, Heather, she was taken to Billings on..." I look to Aaron for help.

"Tuesday. Well, early Wednesday morning, really," Aaron says. "Would you know about her?"

Brandt shrugs. "Sorry. They just don't keep me in the loop on those things. Since I've already got my phone out, let's try to call over there. Maybe we'll be surprised and it will work."

I feel a surge of hope when he says, "It's actually ringing." But my hope plummets when he says, "Nope. Rang once and that was it."

He redials, but it won't connect at all this time.

"Okay." I sigh. "We'll stop by the clinic and check."

"Thanks for passing our message on to Bill," Aaron says, reaching out to shake Brandt's hand. We say our goodbyes and Aaron gently takes me by the elbow. "Ready, Laurie?"

Why would they do that? What could James Riverstone think could be so bad his wife and children are better off dead? Oh, I know we rejoice at the prospect of being in heaven, being with Jesus, but to murder your children, then yourself...

I choke back a sob. Aaron pulls me close as we walk out the door.

Chapter 38

Our walk is at an almost leisurely pace. I wonder if we look like two people in love, simply taking a stroll. There's little talk on our walk; both of us are lost in our own thoughts. The murders of Dan Mansen and the people at Aaron's apartment, along with the suicides, are beyond my comprehension. What's happening to my town?

We finally reach the dojang. As soon as we open the door, we immediately know something's wrong. The smell is completely wretched.

"Not good," Aaron says, shaking his head.

Turning on his flashlight, Aaron whispers, "Wait here a minute."

"Why?"

"I just want to make sure no one came in while we were gone."

"Nuh-uh. I'm going with you." We check out the training area, the office, and both locker rooms. All the shower stalls have a standing, brown, slimy, waterlike substance. The toilet bowl water has evaporated to almost nothing, and what's left is the same brown goop.

"I don't think we can stay here tonight," Aaron says.

"Yeah, no way. Not with it like this. Can we use the plunger to get it to go down?"

"If it was only the sewer lines to the studio, maybe. But most of the town is probably having the same problem. My guess—and really, it's only a guess—is until the power comes back on, this is going to continue."

"So, um, I need to use the bathroom," I say sheepishly.

He stares at the toilet for a minute, then says, "We could try something like when we hike up by Ten Sleep. You know, everything needs to be hauled out of there, even human waste."

"Yeah, I know. And *that*, Mr. Aaron Ogden, is why I don't hike around there."

He gives me a patient smile. "So we do our thing and then bag it up."

"What exactly do you have in mind?

"Same idea, only we put the bag in the toilet so you're nice and comfortable. Then, um, afterward, we seal it up."

I close my eyes and shake my head. "If we must."

"Can you give me five minutes?"

I motion with my hands for him to do what he needs to do.

He turns and leaves the locker room. I follow him so I can put some distance between me and the smell. Taking my backpack off, I set it against the wall in the training room. I'd love a workout. Maybe we can set up some lights and make it happen. I slip off my shoes and socks, then stretch out on the mat.

After a couple of minutes, Aaron tells me it's ready. I stop by my locker and pull out my shower shoes before heading to the toilet section. No way am I going barefoot in there today.

He's happily showing off his handiwork: a garbage bag secured under the toilet rim. "I think we should use this for the day. I filled this bucket with leftover sand, you know, from that heavy bag we had donated?"

Oh, I do know about that heavy bag. We were very thankful to get it. One of ours was splitting at the seam, and another local business donated the bag and a few other things for a mention in our last tournament. I bought the sand to fill the round base at the bottom, but I got way more than we needed and overfilled it to the point it couldn't be moved. Oops.

I nod as he says, "Sprinkle sand over it after you...you know, do your thing. Then close the lid. The hand sanitizer is already on the counter."

I scrunch up my face to show what I think of this. Aaron shrugs and leaves the room.

After I *do my thing*, I find Aaron in the office. He's leaning back in the chair, fingers laced behind his head, staring at the ceiling.

"Hey."

"Hey yourself," he says, sitting upright and giving me a smile.

"What are you doing?"

"Thinking we should walk to Bill's place."

"Yeah. It's, what, five miles?"

"A little over six from here."

"So only a couple of hours to get there?"

"Right. It shouldn't be too bad."

"Should we take the rifles and duffle bags?"

"I don't think so. We'll leave them in the lockers. As soon as we get there, I'll bring my truck back for them, maybe empty out most of the usable stuff from here. We'll keep a few emergency things stashed in case we need to stay here again. But overall, I think we'll be safer at Bill's place."

"Until we can get back into your apartment?"

He purses his lips and nods morosely.

"Let's go, then. The sooner we get some fresh air, the better."

"Let me use the…um, you know, then we'll get going."

"The bathroom, Aaron? Why are you blushing? You think I think you don't go to the bathroom?" I tease.

With a smile, he shakes his head before disappearing into the locker room.

Chapter 39

We leave a note for Master Shane in case he stops by the dojang. Aaron attaches it to his own locker with a magnet, their usual way of leaving notes for each other. It simply says, "Visiting Freckles."

I asked him why he didn't write "gone to your place" or something that was clear where we are. He shook his head and said, "I don't know. Just doesn't seem smart to advertise where we are. Only someone who knows him knows Freckles, so…"

Seems logical. Paranoid, but logical.

Our walk is completely uneventful. We make great time, stopping only to rehydrate, and arrive in less than two hours. Freckles is in the house, barking his head off. Master Shane isn't home.

"Hey, Freckles, just your buddies, Aaron and Laurie," I say.

His bark changes in pitch at the sound of my voice, soon turning into a whine. I envision him on his back looking for a tummy rub. Of course, with the windows covered in plywood, I can't look in to see exactly what he's doing.

"You hungry?" Aaron asks.

"Famished."

"Let's heat up one of the cans we salvaged from the fire. A few of them are the right size to be baked beans."

We look over the fire items laid out on the porch. I point to one and say, "That one looks like spaghetti sauce. This one here—" I point to a different can "—might be baked beans, but I'm not sure."

"Okay, we'll try this one," he says, picking up the one I think is baked beans.

"And if I'm wrong and it's spaghetti sauce?"

"Tomato soup." He gives his goofy smile.

I can't help but laugh. "Okay, yeah. That's fine."

He opens the can with a tiny little can opener. I watch as he makes it look easy to operate. I have one in my pack too, but I'm not sure how to use it. As soon as the lid is partway, a bean lifts up slightly.

"What? No tomato soup?" I joke.

"Maybe next time."

He uses the can as a pot, heating it on his small stove. We each have a collapsible bowl and a spoon. Freckles is now settled, so we only hear the occasional whine.

By the time it's finally ready, I'm so hungry I can barely stand it. I dig into the first bite, ready to savor the baked bean flavor. I stop midchew. It tastes…wrong. The beans are mushy and burned, maybe even a little sour.

I look at Aaron; he spits his mouthful back in his bowl. "Don't eat it, Laurie."

I spit mine out also. "What happened? The fire ruin it?"

"I guess so. It must have gotten so hot it cooked in the can. I didn't even think about that happening."

"It's all ruined? Every can?"

"Probably…yes. That's my guess. Maybe the ones with the labels still on are okay, but…" he lets out a huge sigh, "we can't risk it. We can't risk getting sick."

I set my bowl aside. "We should've brought the duffle with the food in it."

"We'll go back for it. But we'll eat first. We each have two dehydrated meals in our backpacks, plus an assortment of the energy gels and beans my dad bought for trail running. Let me start boiling water, and we'll have one of the meals."

"What should I do with the overly baked beans?"

"Can you dump it in Bill's burn barrel? That way Freckles won't get into it."

My dehydrated meal—kale and white bean stew—is fine. A little bland, but not terrible. The convenience of being able to simply heat water, then rehydrate it and eat it out of the bag makes up for the blandness.

After we eat, Aaron asks, "Do you want to stay here and rest on the porch while I go get our stuff?"

"How long will you be?"

"I'll go to the dojang first, then I thought I'd see what I could find out about my apartment."

"I don't want to stay here alone," I say, hefting my backpack onto one shoulder.

What took us two hours on foot should only take us about five minutes in Aaron's truck. Before we leave, he unhooks the utility trailer and empties the items we salvaged from the house out of the truck bed, securing everything in Master Shane's large barn.

Master Shane's property is pretty amazing. It was part of an old working sugar beet farm, before it was broken up into pieces and sold. When it was divided, they sectioned the pieces into long rectangles, with one of the short edges bordering the road.

The barn is a relic from the pre-beet-farm days when this place was an actual subsistence farm. The foundation of the original house is near where he built his place.

Both of the buildings are close to the road. Master says, in hindsight, he wishes he would've put the house on the other side of the barn to give a little more privacy. Not that any road in Prospector County is overly busy, but he does see river traffic with the public access spot being less than half a mile from his house.

Of course, that was before we had the fuel issues we're now facing. I suspect it won't be long until driving is a thing of the past—at least temporarily until our president or whoever can fix things.

"Can we try the radio?" I ask.

"They only update at 7:00 pm now. The Prospect station does 7:00 am, but you know how hard it has always been to get that one to come in here in Wesley."

"How do you know?"

"Brandt Wyatt told me last night."

"Ah, okay." I watch as the houses increase on the edge of Wesley.

"What are they doing about people in jail? The ones who were there when this started?" I ask.

"They let people not deemed a threat to society out, you know, like people with DUIs and drug charges. The others are still in jail, and two of the jailers are living there to care for them. Wyatt and a few of the other jailers have been moved to other places. Since Wyatt lives in Wesley, he's here."

"That makes sense." I nod.

It takes us only a few minutes to empty the dojang of everything we deem essential. Aaron and I each leave our gym clothes and doboks in our locker, along with half a dozen bottles of water and several snack bars—our stash in case we need to spend the night here again.

We take the rifles and the handgun Aaron left here earlier. If someone were to break in, they could use the food and clothing, but the idea of leaving a handgun was something we decided against. What

141

if whoever broke in was someone like the people who attacked Aaron's apartment complex? Or like the person who killed Dan Mansen? No, we didn't want to leave a gun for them.

"That it?"

"Almost." Aaron replies, going into the women's locker room. He returns a minute later carrying a garbage bag tied off at the top.

"Please tell me that isn't what I think it is."

"If you think it's the toilet bag, you're right."

"Ewww. What are you going to do with it?"

He shrugs. "Bury it, I guess."

"Fine, but it rides in the bed of the truck, not the cab."

"Agreed."

Chapter 40

Next, we go to the substation. There are still people loitering, but not as many as earlier. Brandt Wyatt is still manning the desk. If possible, he looks even more exhausted and haggard. His uniform is rumpled, and his thinning hair is going in multiple directions. The odor in the substation is about equal to the dojang. I can't help but wrinkle my nose.

"Pretty bad, isn't it?" Brandt asks.

"It is," Aaron agrees.

"It's really bad in the bathrooms," Brandt says. "I hate even going in there."

"Has Bill been here?" Aaron asks.

A deep frown creases Brandt's face as he nods. "He was here. After I told him about Mansen, he left to go help at your apartment complex. Mostly, I think he wanted to see if he could get info on who they think killed Dan.

"What's happening at the apartments?"

"Mopping it up now."

Aaron noticeably brightens. "That's good. Everyone's okay? Sheriff and police, I mean."

"No fatalities on our end. Couple of very minor injuries is all."

"Can we go there?"

"Not sure you can get in yet. They're using the machine shop parking lot as a staging area. You know the one? Stop there. They'll give you more info."

"Thanks, Brandt. Is someone relieving you soon?"

"We'll see," he says with a grimace. "We're spread pretty thin. Most likely, I'll set up a cot in the back, lock the place up, and wait for people to bang on the door if they need something."

"Why not hook up one of those battery-operated doorbells? I put one in at my apartment, and it works well. They sold them at the hardware store. I heard that place, like every other store, has been picked over pretty well, but maybe he still has them. I can't imagine doorbells would be a hot commodity."

"Probably not. That's a good idea. We did already clear him out of batteries—any we could use. All of our radios are running on batteries. We've made sure to share some with the clinic too. Sheriff Parker is supposed to stop by here when he's free. I'll share your idea about the doorbell."

At the staging area, one of the first people we see is Master Shane. Aaron goes to him, embracing him in a manly sympathy hug. I'm next to offer condolences for the loss of his friend. Though he tries to be stoic, his eyes glitter with unshed tears.

"You have good timing," Master says. "They're going to start letting people in to get their things."

"We can't stay here?" Aaron asks.

"You won't want to stay here."

"Why is that?" I ask, immediately understanding as the memories of the shooting and screaming hits me. "Oh. How many…" I take a breath.

"Seventeen residents, including your next-door neighbor and his wife. Sorry, Aaron. I know you were friends."

Aaron nods. I think he expected Bruno died when we heard the shooting.

"Eight attackers are dead; four surrendered," Master Shane says.

"What will happen to them?" I ask.

"Not sure. Not even sure I want to know. Things might be pretty different these days compared to how it was."

"Meaning?"

"Meaning…you know, never mind. I really have no idea what I'm talking about. So, anyway, you'll need an escort to go to your apartment. Let me see if they'll allow me to take you."

"Did you help here?"

"Not directly, you know, with me being retired and all."

I shrug, and Aaron nods.

"You two will be staying with me, right?"

"We'd appreciate it, sir," Aaron says.

We're allowed in with Master Shane as our escort.

We take both trucks, Aaron's and Master's. Aaron drives an older Ford Ranger Super Cab. It's fine, but not great for hauling large amounts. Master Shane also drives a small truck, a newer Toyota Tacoma.

Parked in front of Aaron's apartment is my car. The back window has been shot out, along with both tires on the passenger's side. Even though my car was nothing special, an older sedan Aaron bought cheap and fixed up for me, it has treated me well. It did great on fuel and was a perfect little college car. I don't even bother to stifle my sigh.

The front door to the apartment is ajar; the wood of the door jamb is fully splintered. I guess I should've expected this, based on what we heard while we were escaping last night. Inside the apartment is a mess. The furniture is overturned, glass is on the floor from where the windows were shot out, and the noxious odor of the sewer system is overwhelming.

"You probably wouldn't want to stay here anyway with the way this place smells," Master says.

"True," Aaron agrees.

We're pleased to find all of our food, water, and other supplies right where we left them. Aaron packs things up from his bedroom and around the house that he wants to take with us.

"I'm going to see what all is in my car that we can use," I say. While I do want to check my car, the smell in the apartment is almost unbearable. "My phone should be in there. I'll try our parents. Maybe we'll get through."

"Good idea," Aaron says. "If you get anyone, can you holler at me? I'd like to talk."

I try both sets of parents several times without connecting. I take my phone and the car charger, moving them to Aaron's truck.

"What was this all about?" I ask Master when he comes out with a load of stuff.

"I think it started as an argument between Aaron's neighbor and his brother-in-law. Then the brother-in-law yapped about it to the wrong people. Those guys turned a minor family squabble into a war."

"Aaron thought he saw the guy that shot at him on the river."

"Could've been. One of the suspects we took into custody said they combined forces with some drifters, people who ended up here after the attacks started."

"Where'd they come from?"

"Not sure. Heard Billings, heard Denver, possible they came from a variety of places and merged into one. Guys like that seem to know how to create a gang."

Aaron decides we should syphon the gas from my car's tank, so we pull his truck up next to my car and top it off using a hose Bill keeps in is toolbox behind the cab. Then we say goodbye for now to his apartment.

Chapter 41

Aaron and I stop at the clinic before returning to Master Shane's house.

Unfortunately, there's still nothing known about Toby, and the last update on Heather was early this morning—she's still in a coma. We do find out that update was made by telephone. Seems the Billings hospital called on the radio and asked if they could try to call someone's cell phone, just to test. The call went through the first time.

As soon as we leave the clinic, at Aaron's request I try our parents again. The calls still won't go through. As we drive out to the house, I realize I was almost numb to the news. While it was good to hear they were able to use the phone, my reaction was less than it should've been. I should've been ecstatic over it, joyous over the fact the phones are coming back.

And on the flip side, I should feel terrible about Heather's injury and Toby still missing. And I do, but it's weird. I feel almost indifferent. I want to cry for those kids, but I can't. I want to cry for Dan Mansen, for the Riverstones, for Bruno and the others at the apartment complex, even for Monica Daniels...but I'm not. I can't.

Is this what it's going to be like now? Am I going to become immune to heartache?

I was sad when I heard about Dan Mansen, but was I as sad as I would've been a week ago?

One week. The planes crashed a week ago today. I had no idea that night how much our lives would change. Will I ever see my parents again?

"You okay, Laurie?" Aaron asks as we pull into Master Shane's driveway.

I close my eyes and lean back on the headrest. "Not really."

"You need a good meal and a good night's sleep."

"No, Aaron," I snap, "I need things back to the way they were. I need them normal. I can't handle this...this...violence—all this death."

"I know," he whispers, putting his hand on my arm, trailing his fingers to my hand.

147

I scrunch my eyes up. Aaron's right. A good meal and sleep. Then, tomorrow, I'll... what? Will everything suddenly improve tomorrow?

All at once, in a rush of emotion, I understand the Riverstone family. Maybe Monica Daniels, too, but mostly the family. I understand why a mom and dad would want to spare their children. What kind of life do we have to look forward to?

Aaron curls his fingers around mine, solid and firm. "Everything is overwhelming right now. A lot has happened in a few days. You and I, we're essentially homeless at the moment. But we're together. And Bill—he'll help us. We'll help him too. He's probably about in the same shape, with losing his friend."

I nod, feeling selfish.

"You ready to go in?"

"Yeah."

As always, Freckles gives me a wonderful greeting. He doesn't know about all of the terrible things going on. I drop to the floor to rub his belly. He squirms and wriggles, begging for more. I can't help but smile.

"Smells amazing in here," Aaron says.

"I thought you'd enjoy a piping plate of spaghetti," Master answers.

Aaron and I look at each other and simultaneously say, "Tomato soup." While we don't exactly burst out laughing, we do both share a small chuckle.

"What's that?" Master asks.

"Nothing, sir," Aaron says.

"I need to do my laundry," I say.

"Tomorrow," Aaron says. "We'll do it first thing. I'll help and it won't take long. Uh, Bill, we need to throw away the food I brought from my parents' house. We tried a can of baked beans and they weren't good."

"I wondered about that; thought they might have boiled in their cans."

"I think I'll burn them in your barrel. Is that okay?"

"Sure. Wait until tomorrow, though. Seems the wind might be coming up. Looks like a storm on the horizon."

During dinner, Master Shane says, "We need to set up a watch schedule."

"Sir?" Aaron asks.

"I'm not sure, no one really is, but it's possible Dan's murder was someone we both had dealings with."

"Why do you think that?" I ask.

"There were a few clues left behind, possibly on purpose."

"Why would someone leave clues on purpose?"

"To mess with me. So I'd be sure to know who killed Dan and what he's capable of."

"Can you and I handle the watch tonight, Bill?" Aaron asks. "Laurie needs to get some sleep."

"Absolutely."

"No. Let me help." My protest is weak, even to my own ears.

"You sleep tonight, Laurie. Tomorrow you can help."

Master Shane stares at his plate. Aaron and I share a look and a shrug. After a few moments, Master looks up and says, "I don't think we'll be able to stay here."

"What?" I say, with considerable dismay, while Aaron calmly asks, "Why is that, sir?"

Master lets out a big breath. "Things are bad, probably worse than you two even know. What happened at the apartment complex and to Dan are only two of many incidents. Sheriff Parker won't be able to keep responding. There's some concern about the road between here and Prospect. And they're already advising people not to use the road between here and Bakerville. A few people have been attacked; one guy went missing. Of course, some people think he isn't really missing, and just doesn't want to be found.

"But anyway, Wesley will still have the city police and the two sheriff deputies who live here. Oh, and Brandt Wyatt. That's it. Whatever happens will be up to them."

"What about you, sir? Are you out of retirement?"

"Nope. Sheriff asked; I declined. As much as I still feel a duty to my community and county, there's reasons I'm not going back to the department."

"Such as?" I ask.

"For one—you two. We're family, always have been, but especially now."

Aaron starts to say something, but Master holds up a hand. "That isn't the only reason, but all I'm willing to say tonight."

Aaron nods.

"And why can't we stay here?" I ask.

149

"I think we'll need a twenty-four-hour watch. Not just today, but every day until law and order can be reestablished. With only three of us, that's not possible. I would've asked Dan to come here, but..." He lets out a loud sigh. "Even so, even with four people, it wouldn't be sustainable."

"We could do eight-hour shifts," I say. "That's no different than a job."

"It would be way different than a job," Master says kindly. "You'd have to pay attention 100 percent of the time—eight hours a day, day in and day out, without a day off. At some point, it'd be a recipe for disaster. One of us would fall asleep on duty, and if it's the wrong time..." He shakes his head. "We can't do it. Which reminds me, we need to make sure you two are properly armed. You'll need to carry your sidearms at all times. And let's keep the shotguns handy. You each have your knife?"

"My pocketknife, sir," Aaron says, "the one I showed you a few days ago. I didn't give Laurie one yet, but I brought the ones I had in my apartment."

"I'll give you a boot knife too," Master says. "I have several. Laurie, I'm sorry we didn't make a point of finding you extra clothes and gear. We'll try to do that in the next few days."

"What will we do?" I ask.

"I've been thinking about this. One of my Yongmudo students stopped by the dojang when I was boarding it up. He invited us to his place."

"Who's that?" Aaron asks.

"Jake Caldwell. He said they're set up pretty well. I guess his older kids and their spouses are there too—not Mollie, though. Remember how she was on a business trip last week? She wasn't back yet when I saw him. She was driving home."

"So she should be back by now?" Aaron asks.

"I'd guess so."

"Where do they live?" I ask.

"Bakerville. I'm not entirely convinced we should go there. Like I said earlier, the road between here and there might be dangerous. And while I like Jake and Mollie just fine, I don't know them outside of class. We haven't socialized."

I don't know them at all, so I turn to Aaron and ask, "What do you think of them?"

150

Aaron shrugs. "They've only been taking classes for less than a year. They both try hard, and so does their son. Jake is a natural athlete, so it's easier for him. Mollie, she's..."

"A bit of a klutz," Master says. "But she's a scrapper. And like you say, they both try hard."

"She's a scrapper? What's that mean?"

"We don't have very many women in Yongmudo," Aaron says. "Lots of times, she's the only female on the mat, so she's practicing with the men."

"Yeah, so? It's like that in Taekwondo sometimes too."

"True. But in Yongmudo, we get up close and personal. It's all about self-defense, remember?"

I shrug as he says, "So she's a short, middle-aged female, and some of the guys are afraid of hurting her. She's been known to take advantage of that and has taken more than one of them down when they least expect it."

"Seems she got the better of you one day, too, Aaron," Master Shane says with a wink.

Aaron smiles and shakes his head.

"Okay, but that doesn't tell me what you think of them. Are they trustworthy? And why go there instead of staying here? Just so there's more people to be on guard duty? Is that the life we have to look forward to? Watching and waiting for the next bad guys to attack us?"

I don't realize my voice is increasing in volume with each word, until I yell out, "Because if it is, I don't want that life!"

Chapter 42

Aaron touches my hand. "Hey, it's okay."

"No, it's not okay," I snap. "You two might think this...this Rambo stuff is okay, but I don't. A few days ago, I killed a man. Me! Not you, me. I did it. And now you're telling me I have to be on my guard and ready to kill again? No. I won't do it."

In his very calm, very professional sheriff voice, Master Shane says, "There isn't a choice in this. Our world has changed since those planes were shot out of the sky. Going forward, we have to be on guard."

"Oh, I have a choice. Believe me, I have a choice," I sneer. "Monica Daniels made a choice."

"Enough!" Aaron roars, slapping his hands on the table. "What exactly are you saying? You're thinking of killing yourself?"

I cower slightly. Is that what I'm thinking? I did definitely say words that sounded like that. But am I really thinking of killing myself? I drop my eyes. "I-I don't know. I just can't—how can we live like that, always thinking we'll be in danger?"

Aaron replies, "We live like that by trusting God and trusting in each other. Right now, I can't imagine a world where we're always on guard either. But we know there are always trials. God doesn't tell us it will be easy, but he does tell us he'll be by our sides. He'll be by your side, Laurie, no matter what you're going through. I'll be by your side too."

"Me too," Master adds.

I nod. I believe them, that they'll want to be there for me, but I'm still...I don't know.

"Maybe I really do need to sleep," I say quietly. "What's the verse about things being better in the morning?"

Aaron visibly relaxes. "Weeping may tarry for the night, but joy comes with the morning?"

"No...something about mercies being new in the morning."

"The steadfast love of the Lord never ceases," Master Shane says. "His mercies never come to an end. They are new every morning; great is your faithfulness."

152

I've never heard Master Shane recite scripture before. My mouth must be hanging open, because he says, "What? You think I don't know my Bible?" He winks. "Plus, it's part of a wonderful song. You know, 'Great is Thy Faithfulness.'"

"I-I've never known you to attend church."

He looks at Aaron, then to me. "Aaron and I belong to a men's Bible study group with Pastor Robert. I started over the winter. I hadn't been in church for at least thirty years, but," he shrugs, "I started realizing something was missing in my life. It was the Lord. So, I invited him back."

"Why didn't you tell me this?" I ask Aaron.

"Sorry, Laurie. I thought it was Bill's story to tell."

"So, let's get you set up, Laurie. You can sleep in the loft; that way you'll have the half bath to yourself. I'm sure thankful to be on a septic tank and not on the city sewer system. What a mess they've got with that."

I'm almost in a fog as I get ready for bed. These last few days have been terrible. I keep thinking about all the changes to our lives. And the Riverstone family—I can't get them out of my head.

I try to settle into bed, but my body has a terrible time relaxing. Many times, it jerks for no reason, waking me up. I start thinking of the song Master Shane mentioned, "Great is Thy Faithfulness." I can't remember all of the words, but I remember the tune and the beginning, "Great is thy faithfulness! Great is thy faithfulness! Morning by morning new mercies I see."

Please, God, show me new mercies in the morning.

I must finally fall asleep, because the next time I wake up, the sun is shining. The first thing I think of is the song.

But I don't feel new mercies. Really, it's quite the opposite.

Chapter 43

Master Shane is on the couch in the great room with his left foot on Freckles, using him as a footrest. I watch as Freckles twists slightly, asking for a back rub. Master obliges, muttering, "You're a very spoiled dog." The dog's tail beats against the hardwood in agreement.

Freckles bounces off the floor, causing Master's leg to shoot up, as he runs in my direction. Master laughs and says, "In a hurry there, dog?"

I drop down to greet him, rubbing him behind the ears. He's so easy to please. As long as he gets food, water, and plenty of pets, he's happy.

"How'd you sleep, Laurie? Good?"

His question slams me with a memory of my dad. Every morning during coffee I'd ask, "How'd you sleep?" Every single morning, his answer was, "With my eyes closed."

I can't help but smile. My dad is such a goof with a weird sense of humor. What would he think about all that's happening? If he was home, he'd be doing everything possible to ensure my mom and me were safe. Shoot, Mom would fight right alongside him to take care of me, her little girl.

There's a phrase I hear a lot—cowboy up. It originated from rodeo when a bull or bronco rider was up next. "Cowboy up" meant get ready for your ride. These days, it's commonly used to tell someone to toughen up or be strong.

It's no secret: even when our world was normal, Wyoming had a high suicide rate. Being self-reliant, or cowboying up, helps people thrive in our sometimes-harsh environment. But it can also put people at risk during a personal crisis.

Part of me realizes this is where I am now—seriously at risk. But instead of telling Master, instead of asking for help, I smile weakly and say, "Fine, thank you."

He gives me a strange look. "We should talk."

I take a deep breath. "Not right now."

He nods grimly. "Soon, Laurie. There are things that need—that need to be said."

"Look, I'm sorry I got upset last night. I'm fine now." *A lie?* Maybe.

"Are you? Are you fine?"

I shrug.

"You can always talk to me, Laurie."

I let out a groan. "Yes. I know, Master."

"And please, would you call me Bill? How many times have I asked you to call me Bill?

"Hundreds, sir," I answer with a small, but genuine, smile.

"That's right, so do it already." He returns my smile.

"We'll see, sir. Is Aaron sleeping?"

"He is. Can I make you a cup of coffee?"

"I can make it. Just tell me how you're doing it."

"No bother," he says, getting up. Freckles, of course, thinks whatever is happening is all for his benefit. He shoots me a look, then promptly gives me up for Master Shane.

"Crazy dog," Master mutters, with an expression of pure affection.

While he makes breakfast, I try to call my parents and then Aaron's. I don't reach either. Master Shane offers me the use of his phone, with the same end result.

After coffee, and the most amazing pancakes from one of those just-add-water mixes, I start on my laundry.

I've never washed anything by hand, except underclothes, and it's much more difficult than I anticipated. Doing the jeans is terrible. I start to think again about what my future might look like. Not good. Definitely not good.

Master Shane spends his time organizing things. He avoids telling me exactly why, but I have little doubt he's planning on going to those people's house. Instead, he just says, "It's good to know where things are."

Aaron gets up around two o'clock. At four, we eat canned soup and flour tortillas. While we're eating, Aaron tells me they want me to rest again tonight. Maybe tomorrow night I can share guard duty. Master Shane heads off to bed, with plans to relieve Aaron at 2:00 am.

Like Master, Aaron works on organizing stuff. Not just his stuff but Master Shane's things also. Apparently guard duty just means staying awake all night with a gun in easy reach. Aaron's wearing his pistol and has a shotgun leaning against the kitchen wall.

"So, when do you think we'll leave?" I ask.

He pauses, holding something he pulled out of the cabinet, then calmly says, "All depends. Right now, we're mainly focusing on discovering what we have. Bill thought the sorting and organizing you and I did was smart. We all know it's likely this problem will continue for some time. The things we have now might be the only things we have for a while."

He stares at me for several seconds. "Laurie, the way you were last night—that wasn't okay. If you're really thinking...thinking *that* is an option, we need to address it."

"And then what?"

"What do you mean?"

"I mean, are you going to take me to see a shrink? Get me some mental health help?"

Aaron looks wounded; I soften my tone. "Because I don't think my insurance company will be able to approve those visits right now."

"Maybe Dr. Anderson—"

"You think going to a dentist is what I need?"

"I was going to say, maybe he can help us find someone, a professional we can talk to."

"I sincerely doubt therapists are holding office hours, even though they're probably more needed than ever before."

Aaron nods. "You're probably right. Bill and I—we can help you."

"Oh, really? You have psychiatric skills I'm unaware of?"

"You know I don't, but I do have a heart full of love for you. Bill, though, he does have some specific training."

I tilt my head. "Like how to talk a jumper off a roof? I'll be sure to let him know if I come across any high buildings."

I don't bother to help Aaron with his organizing. Freckles and I sit on the couch, me staring into space and him dozing, only moving when one of us needs to use the bathroom.

Finally, I say, "I'm going to bed."

Aaron pauses his packing and walks over. He pulls me into a tight hug and draws his head back enough to look into my eyes. "I may not have any special psychiatric skills, but I'll help you any way I can."

Tears immediately fill my eyes. "Thank you," I whisper, then lean in to receive my usual chaste goodnight kiss.

156

What he plants on my lips is anything but chaste. My knees go weak and my stomach does a flip.

When he pulls away, he says in a husky voice, "How about talking to Pastor Robert?"

In an equally husky voice, I say, "Yeah, maybe."

"Laurie, once we are...okay, when you're feeling more like yourself, then..." He turns red, takes my hand, and kisses my promise ring. When he does, I notice he's wearing his coordinating band. Both are simple, with a swirl design leading to a cross in the middle and a small, almost microscopic, diamond in the center.

"As soon as we can, we're getting married." He hesitates before continuing, "I'm not making light of what you're feeling by promising you a wedding, but when you feel ready, I'm ready."

I want to squeal at the top of my lungs and yell, *I'm ready! I'm ready!* But I know he's right. I'm teetering on the edge of a cliff. He kisses me again, not quite as robustly as the previous one, but still impressive.

"See you in the morning."

"See you in the morning," I agree.

I climb the stairs. Unlike last night when I was in a complete fog, tonight I notice the detail of the railings. Master Shane did all the interior work himself. The spindles are a fancy twisted rebar with the rail across the top a high polished hardwood he special ordered, then carved to fit. I run my hand along the smooth wood.

At the top of the stairs, the loft railing has a beautiful mountain landscape forged out of iron. He has a small metal working shop, along with a wood working area, in the old barn, and did all the work himself. I allow myself a smile while I admire the beauty of his work.

Lying in bed, I think of the verse about his mercies being new every morning and start humming "Great is Thy Faithfulness."

Tomorrow is a new day—a better day.

Chapter 44

"Laurie. Laurie! Laurie, wake up."

"Hmm? Why?" I ask, trying to rise from my fog. Freckles is barking—not in the house but from outside. Master Shane's face is way too close. "What's wrong?" I ask.

"Shh. You need to get up. Grab your gun and follow me. Stay low."

There's enough of a glow coming from the lanterns on the main floor for me to see easily. Master Shane is fully dressed, including his boots. I slip into my shower shoes and grab the belly band to put on.

"Just take the gun and be ready," Master says.

"Where's Aaron?"

"I don't know. Freckles is outside, so I assume Aaron is also."

We walk hunched over down the steps. As we reach the main level, the room is well lit. Either Aaron or Master Shane made sure to turn on every battery-operated lantern.

"Here's what we'll do," he says. "I'm going out to find Aaron. Bolt the door behind me, and then I want you here." Master motions behind the staircase. "From here, you can see both doors. If anyone other than Aaron comes in, shoot them until they're no longer a threat. No warning—just be sure it isn't Aaron, and shoot. Remember, there could be more than one. I'll yell out before I come in."

"What's happening? Is someone out there?"

"I don't know for sure, but that's my guess."

Freckles's bark is still frantic and combined with growls, but slightly quieter; he's moving farther away from the house. I think there's also a human shout underneath the barking.

Master Shane cautiously steps out the back door. As soon as he leaves, I realize I'm shaking. I take a couple of deep breaths to try and calm down. It doesn't help.

Freckles's bark has changed; it has an intensity I've never heard and is combined with growling. I definitely hear a man's voice yell out something. Then, all noise stops. Is it because he's too far from the house for me to hear him? Or did whatever he was barking at get scared off? I strain to hear more from Freckles.

It's many minutes before Master Shane calls out, "Laurie, it's Bill. I'm coming in. Do not fire. Repeat, do not shoot." I hear the door lock rattle. "Confirm you understand. I'm coming in."

"Okay, I-I understand. I won't shoot." I hold my gun next to my thigh, continuing to be mindful of the trigger.

The door opens; Master Shane is hunched over, his back to me. He glances back and says, "Can you close the door?"

I move over near him. He has Aaron under the armpits, dragging him inside.

I gasp. "What's wrong with him?"

Aaron moans.

"I think someone clobbered him. Found him in a heap at the edge of the house."

"Freckles?"

"Don't know."

I close the door, then help get Aaron to the couch.

"He's bleeding," I say, pointing to his cheek.

"Yeah, grab a towel from the bathroom."

I hustle to the bathroom, grabbing a hand towel, then decide we need a wet washcloth also. As I open the cabinet drawer, a gruff voice says, "Hold it right there, mister."

Chapter 45

My breath turns shallow. The guy who hurt Aaron—he's inside the house. Realization cuts into me like a knife. I didn't lock the door. *Stupid, stupid, stupid.* This mistake could get Master Shane and Aaron killed.

I slide to the wall, handgun at the ready, finger indexed away from the trigger. I'm breathing much too hard as I peer out the slightly open door. With the staircase in front of the bathroom door, I should be hidden. But as loud as my breath is, he could easily hear me. In through my nose, softly out.

I can only see the guy's back. He's tall, as tall as Dan Mansen was, but skinny like a rail and wearing dirty shorts and a black tank top. He's holding his pistol sideways with one hand, like the gangbangers do in movies. He's between me and the couch where Aaron's lying, with Master Shane kneeling next to him. I don't have a clear shot with Master in my backdrop.

"No problem," Master Shane says calmly.

"Throw your gun aside," a second voice orders. I look for the second guy, but my limited field of view doesn't show him. *What if there's more than two?*

I watch as Master Shane sets his handgun on the floor and slides it away.

"Now put your hands up," number two bad guy says.

Master raises his hands. There's a slight moan from Aaron.

"What should we do with them?" gangbanger wannabe guy asks.

"After what their dog did to Paul, we should do the same thing to them," number two answers.

Freckles?

"Where's my dog?" Master asks, still calm but with an edge of steel in his voice.

"Yeah, Eric, let's give them a taste of their own medicine," gangbanger says.

"What does that even mean?" Eric, voice number two, asks.

"I dunno, just thought it sounded good. You know, get back at them for Paul?"

"Okay, yeah. Guess that makes sense."

I need to get out of this bathroom and move behind the staircase where Master had me stationed before. From there, I'll have a full view of the great room.

I squat and duck walk out of the bathroom, making sure I don't move the door as I exit. As soon as I'm in the small hallway, I can see the backs of both bad guys. I look to the back door, the one I neglected to lock, to make sure there isn't anyone else. Good thing there isn't because they'd easily see me. As it is, if these guys turn around, I'm toast.

There's a slight change to Master's face. I think he sees me.

"So, Eric," Master says, with a head tilt in the second guy's direction. I glance at Eric; he's short and squat. No, not squat—fat. His shoulder-length hair glistens with grease. Unlike gangbanger wannabe guy, Eric is holding his weapon with both hands, in triangle stance.

"You mind if I stand?" Master Shane asks. "At my age, my knees aren't what they used to be."

"Oh, your poor knees hurt, old man? Too bad," gangbanger says mockingly.

"Go ahead. Get up," Eric says.

"Thanks, man. I appreciate it," Master says, while pointing at Eric and lifting his eyebrows.

He purposely avoids looking in my direction. Is he sending me a signal? Does he want me to shoot Eric?

Even with my limited knowledge, my gut tells me Eric is the bigger threat of the two. He seems to know what he's doing. But most importantly, where he's standing gives me a clear backdrop should I miss. *I can't miss.* I give Master a nod and get into my own solid isosceles stance, with both hands securing my gun.

"Give me just a second, getting up isn't as easy as it used to be. Don't know how I got so old. Seems to have just snuck up on me one day."

Is this old talk all for show? Watching him at practice, he's still as smooth and dynamic as ever. Slowly, and with plenty of groaning, he starts to stand. I keep my focus on Eric, watching Master in my peripheral.

161

He's fully upright as he bends slowly, saying, "Yep. That position was a little much for me."

He takes a step forward, hands on his hips as he twists his torso. Another couple of steps, playing up his "old decrepit body," and he's within a few feet from the wannabe gangster. He's standing in perfect fighting stance, right leg behind the left. He takes a deep breath and says, "Whew, guess I'm ready now."

"Ready for what, old man?" gangbanger asks. "Ready to meet your maker?"

Master gives a slight chuckle. "You think?"

Then he lets out a roar of a kihap, bends his knees, and drops slightly. Jumping higher than I've ever seen him jump and throwing his rear knee into the air, he delivers an in-to-out crescent kick. He connects with the gangbanger wannabe's hand, sending the gun flying across the room. Wannabe doesn't even seem to realize what's happening as Master Shane slams into him, taking him to the ground.

Eric has his gun aimed at Master as I squeeze my trigger—again and again and again. I watch as each bullet slams into his body. The first one catches him in the right shoulder, not exactly where I was aiming and slightly high. The impact causes him to drop his gun and rotate right. The next shot hits him in the left ribcage. He jerks and rotates again; he's almost facing me now. I fire into his core—two quick shots. He slumps to the ground. He's no longer a threat.

I keep my gun trained on Eric as Master Shane continues his hand-to-hand assault against the other guy. With them on the ground, I can't see exactly what's happening but hear plenty of grunts and groans. Does he need my help? I wait, assuming he'll call out to me.

After what feels like forever, Master Shane breathlessly asks, "Laurie? Is the other guy immobilized?"

I watch as Eric gasps for breath. He's holding his right shoulder with his left hand, trying to apply pressure. The gun is well out of his reach. "He's lying on the ground without his gun," I say.

"Aaron?" Master asks.

"I'm okay," his voice a harsh whisper. My heart aches at the sound.

Master stands, covered in blood, his knife in hand. I watch as thick droplets fall to the floor. He walks over, picks his pistol up off the floor, and then takes four large strides to Eric in the kitchen. I jump at the repercussion from the pistol. *He shot him in the head!*

"Put in a fresh magazine, Laurie," he says calmly, as he steps over and locks the back door.

"Um, it's upstairs. I only grabbed the gun."

"Go. Take care of it."

I race to my room and fumble with replacing the magazine. When I come back downstairs, Aaron's standing, leaning against the couch.

He looks at me and asks, "You okay?"

I feel the tears filling my eyes. My throat aches, and I'm not sure my voice will work.

"Don't fall apart on us, Laurie," Master says, meeting my eyes. "We need to keep it together in case they're not alone."

I swallow hard and whisper, "Okay."

"They were talking about another guy, right?" Aaron asks, swaying slightly.

Master walks over to him and says, "Let's put you in the wingback chair. It gives a good vantage point of both doors. Think you can handle the shotgun?"

"Where's mine?" Aaron asks, sinking into the chair.

"Outside. Surprised they didn't take it from you. I unloaded it but couldn't handle it and you at the same time." Master hands him a shotgun from the closet.

"Where's Freckles? I took him out. I thought he needed to go to the bathroom with the way he was whining and carrying on. I didn't..." Aaron takes a deep breath. "I had no idea there was anyone out there."

"I-I'm not sure," Master says. "I think he might...as soon as it's light, I'll find him."

"You think he might what?" I ask. I'm suddenly cold and shaky.

Master gives me a sad look. "Hold on, Laurie. Let's get you to the couch." I nod as he takes me by the shoulder. Everything starts to dim. I take a deep breath and draw in a mixture of gun powder, blood, and other bodily fluids.

I try a shallow breath through my mouth—no better. My knees buckle.

163

Chapter 46

A rustling starts to pull me out of my fog. The smell of bleach burns my nose. Master Shane is on his hands and knees scrubbing the floor with a white bar towel pink with blood. Aaron's asleep in the wingback chair, shotgun propped against the wall. The lanterns are still lit, but with the windows boarded up, that doesn't mean much. I squeeze my eyes tight as the memories from earlier come rushing back.

The rustling stops and Master Shane asks, "You okay now?"

"Did I faint?"

"Guess you did."

"Freckles?"

"It's just breaking dawn. As soon as it's lighter, I'll find him."

"Where are the...you know...the..."

"Dead guys? On a tarp by the door. I'm going to finish cleaning up, then I'll haul their sorry...carcasses outside."

"Did you try the phone? Can you call Brandt at the sheriff's station?"

"It wouldn't connect. I tried a text, but I'm not sure if he got it."

"Can you use your radio?"

"I only have a scanner. I can listen to some of their talk but can't add my own."

"Do you think Freckles is okay?"

He lets out a big sigh. "No, Laurie, I don't suppose he is."

The tears run out of my eyes and into my ears. So much for things being better in the morning. And now, one of the few bright spots in this awful world is likely gone too. I was stupid to have any hope things would be okay.

I curl into a ball with my face against the back of the couch. I alternate between crying and dozing. After a while, Master Shane wakes Aaron. He needs him to go with him, to watch his back while he looks for Freckles.

Next, he comes over to me. "Laurie."

"I'm not going," I whisper.

"No. No, you should stay here. But you need to either move to the chair Aaron was in or back behind the staircase."

"Why?"

"In case someone tries to get in."

"We already killed them."

"We don't know for sure. There could be others."

"You know, it doesn't really matter to me. I'm staying right where I am."

"We should let her sleep," Aaron says. "We'll lock the door and pray she'll be fine. We'll be back as quick as we can. Laurie, remember what we talked about. We'll get through this."

"You mean like Freckles did?" I snap.

Aaron sighs. "Try to remember you aren't the only one who loved that dog."

Oh, so he thinks I'm being selfish? Ha. *Thanks for your understanding.* I want to lash out; instead, I curl tighter. He touches my shoulder. A few moments later, I hear the soft snick of the lock. After they leave, I sit up.

There's still a slight pinkish tint to the hardwood where Master Shane knifed the guy. So, this is it, huh? There's no place safe. After I shot Eric, I could've turned the gun on myself. I swallow hard. *Do I really want to die?*

I feel my head shake. I don't want to die, but I do want a normal life. I want to finish school, marry Aaron, and go on to dentistry school. Then come back to Wesley and go into practice with Dr. Anderson. After a year or two, Aaron and I will have a couple of kids. That's the dream I've had for years—since long before Aaron and I started dating, when the husband was a nameless, faceless person. But now...now that's all gone.

I'm not going back to school. I won't be a dentist. I'll probably never see my parents again. And Aaron and I can't have babies. I won't bring a child into this world—a world where we're never safe, where even a sweet dog isn't safe.

I think again of the men we killed. I don't mind so much that they're dead. I have little doubt they would've killed Master Shane and Aaron. While I may not want to continue living, it's different for them. I love them both so much and wouldn't want either to die.

165

I look around the room. The shotgun is gone. Where's my pistol? Would Aaron have taken them, thinking I'd harm myself? Another glance around and I see the shotgun by the door.

I recline back on the couch, resting my head against the cushion. I spend several minutes just lying back, thinking of little. The rattle of the door stirs me, but not enough for me to bother sitting up and seeing who it is. If it's another bad guy breaking in to kill me, he'd be doing me a favor.

Aaron steps into my view. His eyes are red and his face is etched in a deep frown.

"We found him. We found Freckles."

I expect the knowledge of actually finding Freckles to slam into me, the grief to hit me hard. Instead, it's more numbness. That seems to be the main thing I feel these days. Nothing.

"We found another guy too. Bill recognized him, thinks it might be the person who killed Dan Mansen. Freckles killed him before—" he gulps "—before those guys...I came in to get a blanket and his dog bed."

"How?"

"What?"

"How'd Freckles kill him?"

"Oh, well, that...he did it protecting us."

"Duh, Aaron. I know that part. I'm asking how our sweet dog killed someone."

"This isn't something you need to know."

"Why not? Think I can't handle it? How did Freckles kill a man, and how did Freckles die? I want to know."

Aaron walks to the couch. Kneeling in front of me, he reaches for my hands. I pull them out of his reach. He sighs and rests his hands on my knees. "You really need to know this?"

Without meeting his eyes, I nod.

Another sigh. "Freckles managed to get the guy on the ground. Then he went at his throat."

"He's an amazing dog," I whisper.

"He loved us."

"Did those...monsters...shoot him?"

"No," Aaron's voice drops to a whisper. "They—can you just remember him the way he was? You don't need the details."

"Did he suffer?"

166

"We don't think so. Bill is digging a grave for him. I'll come and get you when we're ready to, uh, say goodbye."

I nod woodenly. Yes, I do want to say goodbye.

After we bury Freckles, Master Shane takes the bodies of the three dead men into town. While he's gone, Aaron works on the packing. We're leaving tomorrow to go to their Yongmudo student's home in Bakerville. I don't help. I spend my day on the couch, alternating between staring at the wall, staring at the ceiling, and sleeping.

Chapter 47

I didn't bother moving to the loft last night, choosing to sleep on the couch instead. It's Sunday and we should be going to church. So much has changed in a week.

Last Sunday—which feels much longer than only seven days ago—was the day Mrs. Holland told us about nine meals to anarchy. I didn't really believe it could be possible. Not in Wesley, anyway. Maybe in the cities or other towns, but not my town. I was wrong.

When Master Shane returned from town yesterday, he said things are terrible in Wesley. The hospital clinic has shut down, and even though Brandt Wyatt is still manning the sheriff substation, they aren't really responding to calls. The one bright spot is the phones seem to be working better. Even though Aaron and I haven't been able to connect with our parents yet, this news gives me a small glimmer of hope.

If the phones are coming back, will the electricity follow? Our life would be so much easier with electricity. Maybe people would feel less crazy and desperate. Of course, we'd still have the issue of food, but there's a fair amount of wildlife around here, plus the rivers and lake have fish.

Bakerville has even more wildlife than we do, with not only resident deer and elk herds but also being a migration corridor. I've even heard they have the occasional moose and a small herd of wild sheep, plus waterfowl and turkey.

My dad would sometimes take me to Bakerville on bird watching expeditions. He especially liked going during the winter when the geese were on the river. He'd take his camera and try to get shots of them taking off and landing.

He said the best days were after a fresh snow. Those were cold days! Even bundled up, I'd be chilly. After we were finished, we'd drive up the mountain behind Bakerville and stop at the ski lodge for lunch and a hot cocoa.

A few times, my dad went turkey hunting with one of his friends along Little Snake Creek, one of the creeks feeding the river.

Bakerville is a farming and ranching area with a fair amount of cattle and several food crops, including corn, barley, and sugar beets, among others.

Maybe Bakerville will be a good place for us—a place we can be safe until the power returns.

"You're awake," Aaron says.

I nod and ask, "How are you? Head hurt?"

"Not much."

There's a small Band-Aid on his cheek from the cut—the one I was getting a washcloth to clean up when Eric and the other guy waltzed in. I found out later he also has a cut on the back of his head where they hit him.

"Coffee?" he asks.

"Yes, that'd be good. Are we leaving today?"

Aaron nods. "In a bit. Bill is finishing loading."

"What time is it?"

He looks at his watch. "After 8:00. I have your phone on the charger in my truck. I wanted to get you a full charge. I tried calling both our parents but couldn't get through."

I nod. "So, what? We'll stay in Bakerville, until when? Until the lights come back on?"

"I don't know. We'll stay there until it's safe to come back to Wesley. None of us know when that will be."

"But if the phones are working again, it makes sense the power will come back, right?"

"I don't know." He shakes his head. "Things like this..." He swings his arms wide in an all-encompassing gesture. "This hasn't happened before. We don't know what to expect."

"I just don't want to get stuck living with people I don't know."

"Is your backpack ready? And your clothes?" he asks, changing the subject.

"What time are we leaving?"

"No later than 10:00."

"I'll be ready. Mind if I eat first?"

"How about instant oatmeal?"

I shrug as he lights the camp stove under the teakettle. After breakfast, I take my time getting my things together. Aaron gives me a garbage bag for my meager clothing collection. I repack my backpack to make sure it's ready, should we find ourselves on foot. Aaron brings

169

me food items, replacing the dehydrated meal I ate the other day and adding extra marathoner gels, beans, and bars.

"Is your water full?" he asks.

"Yep. And I have my water straw thing."

He nods. "Okay, good. That water straw is an important part of your pack. If something happens and we find ourselves wandering around between here and Bakerville, we'll at least have filtered water."

"You think there's much water between here and there? You know they call it the Wastelands for a reason. It's pretty barren."

"On the surface it seems like a dry desert, but there are a few small streams and several manmade ponds set up for watering stock."

"Huh. I didn't know that. So with streams, we could have fish?"

"Not those kinds of streams. These are more like irrigation ditches moving the water from the reservoirs. Unless a reservoir is stocked with fish—and I don't know of any in the Wastelands that are—then no fish."

"Oh, okay. That makes sense, I guess." I bite my lip. Having access to water is good, but food would be nice too. Of course, there's plenty of deer and antelope. They're just not as convenient for making into a quick meal as fish are.

"We'll be fine. Don't worry. We're just about ready. Bill's strapping the bikes in and making sure the quad is secure. It's good he has a large trailer. We have it loaded pretty full."

"Are we taking all the dirt bikes?"

"Yes, plus the bicycles, skis, snowshoes...everything. We thought Jake and his family might be able to use them. We're also bringing all the guns, food, camping gear, bedding...lots more. Pretty much anything we think has a use. The utility trailer and bed of my truck are overloaded. We don't want to show up there empty handed."

"Okay," I say, not really caring.

"And, Laurie, they have a small farm—chickens, goats, some other livestock, I don't know what all. And a garden."

"Okay? So?"

"We'll need to help on the farm."

"What do you know about farming, Aaron? What do I know about it?"

"We'll learn. We'll earn our keep."

I don't even try to keep from rolling my eyes. "I don't know these people. How do we even know this is the right thing to do? What if they're just looking for manual laborers? We might be nothing more than indentured servants."

A smile plays at his lips. "You have a wild imagination today."

"But I could be right. You don't know."

"I know Jake and Mollie. I'm pretty sure we'll be okay. Let me take your clothes bag out. I have the perfect spot to put it. Check if you have anything else or if there's anything still in the house you think we need."

I check the loft for anything I may have missed, then decide to move through the house room by room. Opening a drawer in the bathroom, I find a nail care kit. I look at my fingers and see my nails are a ragged mess. This kit is going with me.

I wonder what taking care of goats is like? I had a friend in school who had goats. They stunk bad. I suppose we'll be drinking goat's milk. I can't help but make a face.

In the guest room, I find a basket with little soaps and shampoos from hotels. Opening the closet, I discover a waffle-weaved robe and a pair of slippers—both are the kind you might use at a fancy spa. This robe is going to be a new addition to my terribly sparse wardrobe—so are the slippers. I hesitate before going into Master Shane's bedroom. Maybe I'll check the kitchen first.

I'm stooped down, checking a bottom cabinet in the kitchen, when the back door opens and Aaron starts yelling. "Laurie! Laurie! Where are you?"

"Here," I say, popping up.

"We've got to go. Grab your things. We have to leave now."

"Why? What's happening?"

Aaron reaches for a garbage bag lying on the counter and starts shoving my robe and other things inside. "Your backpack?" he asks frantically.

"In the loft," I say, heading to the stairs.

"Here, take this." He thrusts the bag toward me. "Go to the truck. I'll get your pack and be right there."

"What's happening?" I ask again, as he runs up the stairs.

"I'll tell you when we're on the road. Hurry!"

I go out the door, meeting Master Shane at the bottom of the steps. "What's going on?"

"My phone just went off—yours too. There's a notice of a missile attack," he says much too calmly.

"A missile? We're being bombed?"

"Seems like we might be."

"What do we do?"

"We leave now, to go to Bakerville. Jake told me he has a small basement. We'll be safe there."

"We have time to get there?"

"No time to waste, so let's get a move on."

"Where are you going?"

"To grab a couple of things from my room."

I watch as he goes into the house. A missile…like a nuclear bomb? If that's really happening…I set the bag on the ground. The lights aren't coming back on. Our lives are over.

I start walking. Master Shane is less than a half mile from the river. It's still high and swift from the mountain runoff. I'm on the road when Aaron runs up, grabbing my arm.

"Where are you going?"

"Doesn't matter. We're all dead now. We can't survive a nuke attack." I jerk my arm out of his grip.

"Yes, we can! But we have to leave now."

I take off running—only half a mile to the river. Before I make it a dozen feet, Aaron has me in a bear hug, dragging me backwards. I stomp on his foot. My tennis shoes are no match for his heavy work boots. I struggle against his grip, to no avail.

"What's going on?" Master Shane yells.

"She's—Laurie's not okay," Aaron yells, as he continues dragging me backwards.

The next thing I know, Master Shane is next to us, snapping a bracelet around my left wrist. *That's weird.* I look down at it as he snaps a second one around my right. The silver bracelets have a small chain between them.

Handcuffs? He's put handcuffs on me?

"No! No! No!"

"Stop it, Laurie," Master says firmly, using his cop voice.

"I'm not going."

"Laurie, you're putting all of us in danger. Do you honestly think Aaron will leave you here? That I'd leave you here?"

I drop my shoulders, stop fighting, and let them usher me to the truck. As soon as I'm buckled in—compliments of Aaron since I'm still in handcuffs—Aaron runs around and starts the truck. I watch as

172

Master Shane races back and grabs the bag I dropped in the driveway. The next thing I know, we're roaring down the road. I feel myself crying but don't care enough to do anything about it.

We take the side roads and avoid Wesley. I don't pay much attention to where we are. There's some sort of banging noise. Maybe the truck is backfiring? Aaron yells something, but I can't seem to understand.

I turn to look at him; he pushes me down. "They're shooting at us," he yells.

I shrug. *So?*

They'd be doing me a favor if they hit me. Even after the shooting stops, I stay lying on the seat. Aaron strokes my hair. "You'll be okay, Laurie. You will. We'll all be okay."

I close my eyes and drift off. I'm not asleep but not awake either. Am I losing my mind? If I was losing my mind, would I know it?

The truck is slowing down. "What now?" Aaron moans as we coast to a stop. "Sit up, Laurie. Something's wrong."

Chapter 48

I reluctantly sit up and glance around. We're pulled off on the side of the road, just across the highway on the edge of Bakerville. Master Shane is parked in front of us.

"Why'd you stop?"

"I didn't. The truck just quit." He turns the ignition. Nothing happens, not even a click or any sort of response.

"Great. Something else," I mutter, rattling my handcuffs.

Aaron gets out. Master Shane exits his truck too. Aaron pops his hood. After only a few seconds, he slams it shut, shaking the entire pickup. His watery eyes meet my dry eyes through the windshield.

I want to shout out and ask what's wrong, but most of me doesn't even care. I've always cared about what others are feeling or experiencing, but not today. Uninterested, I watch as Master Shane and Aaron do something at Master's jam-packed utility trailer. After a couple of minutes, they roll the quad off, then one of the dirt bikes.

Master fires up the quad; they nod and smile at each other, then Aaron starts the bike. With both off-road vehicles running, they start strapping things to the cargo rack on the quad. Every few seconds, one of them looks in my direction. Aaron pulls a blue tarp out of the bed of the Toyota, then spreads it over the load on the back of the quad.

Even though it's still early in the day, I'm getting warm in the cab. I want to roll down the window, but with the truck off, it doesn't work. I open the door to bring in a little air. They don't seem to hear the door open.

Should I leave?

There's a river running through Bakerville too. Not the same river as we have in Wesley, but it, too, should be swollen and swift with mountain runoff.

How far is it from here? Two or three miles maybe? I shake my head. They'd just stop me as they did before. I'll bide my time and wait until later.

Aaron must have noticed my open door; he gestures, then swiftly walks to me.

"You okay?" he asks.

I glare at him.

"Right. So we're going to need to take the bike. You'll ride behind me. Bill is going to..." He swallows. "Bill will take the handcuffs off so you can put on your backpack. Once we're on the bike and you have your arms around me, we're refastening them."

I roll my eyes and scowl. Aaron just looks sad.

"Go ahead and step out. I'll get our packs from the back seat."

I stand there, not really caring what happens next, as Aaron adds his backpack to the cargo rack of the quad.

Master Shane walks over to me. "Ready, Laurie? We have to get moving, and I can't deal with any of your shenanigans right now. Once we get there, and this immediate crisis passes, we'll get you help. You *will* be okay. You are a warrior. Remember that."

Am I a warrior? No, I'm a hot mess.

He unhooks the cuffs, helps me put my pack on, and walks me by the elbow to Aaron, who's already on the bike and waiting. Once I'm settled behind him, with my helmet on and my arms around his stomach, the handcuffs are put back on. I vaguely wonder about the safety factor of being chained to Aaron.

Master Shane climbs on his quad, and we tear off down the road. Within a few minutes, we're on the bridge crossing the fast-moving river. I consider launching myself off of the bike and over the edge, but I'm connected to Aaron.

A few more minutes and we slow, turning off of the pavement and on to a washboard gravel road. Instinctively, I hold Aaron tighter. After several minutes of bouncing and breathing the dust stirred up by the quad, Master Shane pulls over. We stop behind him as he walks back to us.

Over the roar of the engine, he says, "Laurie, I'm going to release the cuffs. I'd prefer to not have to explain why we have you handcuffed. Can I trust you for the few minutes it will take to get to their house?"

I've resigned myself to finding a good opportunity. Maybe it will happen in the next few minutes. Maybe tomorrow. Maybe next week. I nod and he removes the cuffs.

Moving again, we bounce over a cattle guard and turn up a steep hill. We slow as we reach a driveway. There are two guys there, one swinging the gate closed and the other holding a gun—not exactly

175

pointed at us but ready to swing in our direction. A quick glance shows several other armed men.

Could I? What do they call that? Suicide by cop? Is it the same thing when it's just some armed guy protecting his family? No. That would be stupid. Aaron could get hurt.

Master Shane raises his hands; Aaron follows suit. "Raise your hands, Laurie," Aaron says. I don't bother. Maybe they'll...

"Jake!" Master yells over the quad engine. "It's Bill Shane."

The guy shutting the gate raises his hand in a wave and swings the gate open, gesturing for us to drive in. He hollers to the others, "They're friends."

We slowly follow Master into the yard as the gate is closed behind us. I turn and watch as he locks it and then runs up next to Master Shane, talking and motioning as we go down the driveway, showing us where to park.

Aaron turns off the dirt bike and whispers, "We'll be okay, Laurie. We'll be safe here, and we'll get you some help."

"Laurie, this is Jake Caldwell," Master Shane says.

I stare straight ahead as Aaron says, "Jake, thanks for letting us join you."

"Of course," he says. A flurry of introductions follows; I don't even bother to pay attention. Aaron holds me by the elbow.

"We need to get downstairs," says a man in his midsixties with white hair, a full white beard, and even stark-white bushy eyebrows. Barely visible under the craziness of his brows are kind, brown eyes. In a deep, Texas drawl, he says, "I'm getting nervous, and Betty is probably beside herself."

He looks directly at me. "Pleased to meet you, young lady. I'm David Hammer. What can I carry for you?"

"We really only need our backpacks," Master Shane says. "I think the things on the quad are fine for now with the tarp over it."

"All right, then. It's definitely time to get downstairs," Jake Caldwell says. "Master Shane—"

"Please, call me Bill."

"Okay, sure. Mollie is already in the basement."

"Glad she made it home," Aaron says.

Jake nods. "Me too. She's, uh, had a hard time. We've had some problems. Yesterday, Mollie and three of our daughters were attacked. Our youngest girl is in bad shape." His eyes fill with tears.

"I'm so sorry," Master Shane says.

Jake wipes at his eyes. "Yeah, we're praying she'll be okay. Mollie was hurt too. She's physically going to be fine, but…" he lets out a sigh, "she's not quite herself. She had an incident on the way home too, so it's all been a bit much for her. Just don't be surprised if she's not the Mollie you know."

"I understand," Master says, while Aaron moves his hand from my elbow to interlace with my fingers.

"Mollie's not the only one a mess these days," David Hammer says. "Many are having a hard time."

Then he looks directly at me and says, "None of us are alone in this. We'll put our trust in God, instead of relying on our own sinful nature. He'll make our path straight. With God in the lead, we'll all work together, and not only will we survive but we'll thrive."

He places his hand on my shoulder. "You'll thrive, Laurie."

Epilogue

I'm grateful for the large sunhat my new friend Sarah loaned me. Spending so much time outside these last couple of weeks has given me a slight tan, but, as evidenced by the red tinge to my nose, I'm still susceptible to sunburns.

I move on to a second patch of cactus. Kelley Hudson showed me how to harvest the leaves. She said it's plains prickly pear, and while smaller than the prickly pear growing in the southwest, it's edible and even tasty.

They're also incredibly spikey. Even with gloves on, I've managed to receive many pokes. The Caldwells have been rebuilding their soil and watering quite a bit, so the cactus on their land isn't as plentiful as on the section of public land bordering their property. I've started on the BLM land and will move back to the homestead after this.

Even with a decent-sized garden, vines, fruit trees, and small livestock, I know there are concerns about having enough food for everyone living here. If we can do some wild harvesting, we can stretch the supply. Even in the high desert of Wyoming, there are edibles growing wild—more than just cactus. Kelley says she'll take me exploring so we can find lambs quarter, comfrey, yucca, juniper berries, and several other things she knows grows here.

We already have our eye on several patches of cattail; some were transplanted around the water features on the Caldwells' homestead. The marshes near the river have an abundance of the spikes. Apparently, cattails are sometimes referred to as the supermarket of the swamp, so many parts are edible or useful in some way.

I've been spending quite a bit of time visiting with Kelley—a retired psychiatric nurse practitioner—when she comes over here to check on her "official" mental health patient. I'm an unofficial patient, I guess. I'm not the only unofficial patient. There are several of us living on the farm in need of a friendly ear.

We spent several days in the basement when we first arrived, awaiting fallout from nuclear bombs. Those were terrible days.

Everyone was nice enough and tried to make me feel welcome, but I had a one-track mind.

Especially after I found out why our pickup trucks stopped running.

There was an electromagnetic pulse. I remember the hoopla over EMPs when it was in the news that North Korea could set one off high in our atmosphere and wipe us out. Even though I'd heard of it, I didn't really understand what it was. Master Shane tried to lessen the details and severity when briefly explaining, but he couldn't keep it from me for long.

The EMP was all anyone talked about while we were holed up together.

Aaron wouldn't let me out of his sight, for fear of what I might do. Even taking me with them to get everything from the trucks and trailers. On the way back to the Caldwells' homestead, we found three young children and their very sick mom. The children were dirty, hungry, and scared. But even then, the youngest looked at me with big beautiful eyes and gave me a smile. Finding those little kids gave me a glimmer of hope.

After several days with no radioactive fallout, the general consensus was it was safe to move back aboveground. I've been helping take care of the children we found, along with helping Madison—another lady who has found herself here—with her baby. Madison lives in the cabin I'm staying in and is another one of Kelley's unofficial patients. So is Sheila.

Until a few days ago, I was really concerned about Sheila. So concerned, I stopped thinking how bad my own life had become and focused on helping her get out of her funk.

I don't think she's cured—I don't think I'm cured either—but she seems to be doing better. Talking with Kelley and being friends with Madison and Sheila has helped me considerably.

And, of course, Aaron. He's been wonderful.

Things aren't perfect. We still live in a devastated world. We have some considerable comforts here, though—including solar power—making things feel slightly normal. And thankfully, the toilets flush fine.

In addition to helping with the children living here, I help with the animals and garden. Even though I'm no farmer, it's not as bad as I expected. And I do want to, as Aaron said, earn my keep.

We're also all involved in the community militia. At first, Aaron and Master Shane didn't want me to participate. I know they feared I'd harm myself. And maybe, in those first days, I considered it. But I have things to offer and convinced them I should, at the very least, help teach martial arts. While Taekwondo isn't known specifically for self-defense, we're utilizing many parts of it to give our militia options.

It's been just over three weeks since the airplanes were shot down and our world changed forever. We've been living here almost two weeks. Last week, the militia was put to use when the neighbor's house was attacked. Jake and Mollie Caldwell were visiting the neighbors when the attack happened. Six people went up to help, while the rest of us stayed here in case we needed to defend the homestead, to protect the children. It was a hard and stressful time. I felt myself fading a little but managed to keep it together.

Afterward, with the attackers dead and our people uninjured and out of danger, David Hammer had a special Bible study. He started the meeting with a hymn, "Great is Thy Faithfulness." Several of us were in tears by the time the song ended.

In what many have referred to as the apocalypse, I've become closer to God than I've ever been before. In any spare time I have, I'm seeking out his word and wanting to know more about him. I've found hope in his word.

If I'm honest, before our world fell apart, I would've thought someone saying they found hope in God's word was slightly off their rocker. Even though I was raised in the church and my parents are missionaries, I'm not sure I was ever fully invested. I'd never turned from myself and toward God.

So now I guess I've done it—done what Jesus said was necessary. I'm denying myself, taking up my cross, and following him.

This closeness is what my parents have prayed for me for many years. I know they never envisioned it'd take the end of the world as we knew it for me to come to God. And I do wonder if I'll ever see Mom and Dad again. But God has used these catastrophes to draw me near to him.

Kelley has cautioned me—cautioned all of us—that we've all been through a lot. And it's not over yet. We're living through a disaster with no end in sight. It's important we find healthy ways to cope. Even though we're all busy just trying to survive, everyone on the farm and in the community is encouraged to monitor our emotional, mental, and physical health. And we're encouraged to reach out to each other.

In two weeks and two days, Bakerville is having a triple wedding. Katie, one of Jake and Mollie's daughters, is marrying Leo. A retired couple in Bakerville who have been dating for years is the second couple. And Aaron and I are the third.

I can't help but smile. Aaron has been so supportive of me during my time of melancholy. I know there were times he took my sadness personally—a reminder of his time with Tabitha and the loss of Adam.

He has spent time talking with David Hammer. He misses Pastor Robert but has found a new support system in Mr. Hammer. We've even had a marriage counseling session, with three additional sessions scheduled before the ceremony. While the older couple is having the Bakerville pastor perform their service, Katie and I both want David Hammer to help us with our vows.

We questioned the legality of the weddings with the county courthouse being, as far as we know, out of commission. And if it was still functioning, none of us want to take the risk, or use the fuel, to go buy a marriage license. Mr. Hammer pointed out how Biblical marriage has been around a lot longer than state-sanctioned marriage.

Standing up, with my bowl partially filled with cactus leaves, I take a look around. It's beautiful here, nestled against the base of the mountains to the west and a view of the Wastelands to the east.

Thank you, God. Thank you for giving me a second chance.

Have Laurie and Aaron made the right choice going to the Bakerville? Follow their journey in the Havoc in Wyoming series.

182

Thank you for spending your time with the people of Wesley, Wyoming.

If you liked this book, please take a moment to leave a review.

I appreciate you!

Join my reader's club!

Receive a complimentary copy of *Wyoming Refuge: A Havoc in Wyoming Prequel.* As part of my reader's club, you'll be the first to know about new releases and specials. I also share info on books I'm reading, preparedness tips, and more.

Please sign up on my website:

MillieCopper.com

Now Available

Havoc in Wyoming

Part 1: Caldwell's Homestead

Jake and Mollie Caldwell started their small farm and homestead to be able to provide for an uncertain future for their family, friends, and community. They have tried to plan for everything, but they never imagined this would happen.

Part 2: Katie's Journey

Katie loves living on her own while finishing up her college degree, working her part-time jobs, and building a relationship with her boyfriend, Leo. When disaster strikes, being away from family isn't quite so nice, and home is over a thousand miles away. Will she make it home before the United States falls apart?

Part 3: Mollie's Quest

Two or three times a year, Mollie Caldwell travels for business. Being away from her Wyoming farmstead is both a fun time and a challenge. They started their farm to be able to provide for an uncertain future for their family, friends, and community. The farm keeps the entire family busy, meaning extra work for her husband while she's away. This time, while on her business trip, terrorists attack. Her weeklong business trip becomes much longer as she tries to make her way home.

Part 4: Shields and Ramparts

The United States, and the community of Bakerville, face a new threat... a threat that could change America forever. As the neighbors band together, all worry about friends and family members. Have they found safety from this latest danger?

Find these titles on Amazon:
www.amazon.com/author/milliecopper

Coming Soon

Havoc in Wyoming

Part 5: Fowler's Snare

Welcome to Bakerville, the sleepy Wyoming community Mollie and Jake Caldwell have chosen as their family retreat. At the edge of the wilderness, far away from the big city, they were so sure nothing bad could ever happen in such a protected place. They were wrong. Now, with the entire nation in peril, coming together as a community is the only way they can survive. But not everyone in the community has the people of Bakerville's best interest at heart.

Acknowledgments

Thanks to:

Ameryn Tucker my editor, beta reader, and daughter wrapped in one. I had a story I wanted to tell, and Ameryn encouraged me and helped me bring it to life.

My youngest daughter, Kes, graphic artist extraordinaire, who pulled out the vision in my head and brought it to life to create an amazing cover.

My husband who gave me the time and space I needed to complete this dream and was very patient as I'd tell him the same plot ideas over and over and over.

Two more daughters and a young son who willingly listened to me drone on and on about story lines and ideas while encouraging me to "keep going."

My amazing Beta Readers! An extra special thanks to Tim M. for his expertise in firearms and all things that go boom, Ginger B. for her for all her valuable feedback, Marian G. for giving me a fresh perspective, and Judy S. for always saying, "I can't wait to find out what happens next!"

And to you, my readers, for spending your time with the people of Wesley, Wyoming. If you liked this book, please take a moment to leave a review. I appreciate you!

A Note from the Author

In 2014, my life changed forever when someone I love took their own life. Since that time, I've lost two more extended family members to suicide. In the United States, suicide claims the life of approximately 123 people each day, making it the tenth leading cause of death overall. It is the second leading cause of death for young people between the ages of ten and twenty-four.

In my fiction story, Laurie faces many traumatic events in a short time, leading to her rapid downward spiral. In real life, emotional distress can occur with disasters, family conflicts, relationship issues, work or school troubles, and more.

Why my family members made the decision to end their own lives, I don't know. Even if I knew, it wouldn't change the pain of the loss. In many cases, there is no note and there is no outward indication of any problem. We have no answers. Without answers, how can we help someone else who may be struggling?

Suicide is something we need to talk about. In fact, we can't talk about it enough.

If you are struggling, let your friends and/or family know. Or contact The National Suicide Prevention Lifeline at 1-800-273-8255 or chat online at SuicidePreventionLifeline.org.

About the Author

Millie Copper was born in Nebraska but never lived there. Her parents fully embraced wanderlust and moved around a lot, giving her an advantage of being from nowhere and everywhere. As an adult, Millie is fully rooted in a solar-powered home in the wilds of Wyoming with her husband and young son, while four adult daughters are grown and living on their own. Since 2009, Millie has written articles on traditional foods, alternative health, and preparedness—many times all within the same piece.

Millie has penned three nonfiction, traditional food focused books, sharing how, with a little creativity, anyone can transition to a real foods diet without overwhelming their food budget. Her food storage book, *Stock the Real Food Pantry*, was the number one new Amazon Kindle release in its genre when it debuted in January of 2019. The *Havoc in Wyoming* series is her first foray into fiction, using her homesteading, off-the-grid, and preparedness lifestyle as a guide. While this is her first time putting a story into print, the stories have been rattling around in her head for years. What a relief to finally let the stories out!

Find Millie at www.MillieCopper.com
Facebook: www.facebook.com/MillieCopperAuthor/
Amazon: www.amazon.com/author/milliecopper
BookBub: https://www.bookbub.com/authors/millie-copper

Made in the USA
Coppell, TX
17 July 2020

31134385R00121